THE DRAGON'S MUSE

CREATURES & COTTAGES

Elle Sterling

Cover Art and Design: Impyeu

Developmental and Line Editing: Adrienne Lee Seo

Starry Hill Map: fictionsandfriction

To all those lonely hearts looking for a place to belong.
May you find your own Starry Hill.

Content Notes

This book is sweet, cozy, and spicy. It is intended *only* for adult readers 18+.

Should you have any specific questions about triggers, please don't hesitate to reach out to me at elle@ellesterling.com for more details.

If any of the following elements make you uncomfortable, please proceed with caution:

Both Beck and Eleanor are neurodivergent, and as with any disability, this shows up in different ways for them. Even though neither of them has a formal diagnosis, you'll see characteristics of their neurodivergence in Beck's black-and-white thinking and Eleanor's rejection sensitivity. Starry Hill is a very supportive community, and they do their best to accommodate everyone's needs, but both characters have faced some hardships out in the wider world.

Other content to note:

Strong language

Explicit sex between two consenting adults, including in semipublic situations

Nonhuman anatomy and whiskered appendages

Shifted oral sex

Abusive relationship with mother (off page)

FMC working through related parental trauma

Brief mentions of parental abandonment

No contact parents

Rejection sensitivity

Body image insecurity

Pregnancy (not main characters)

Starry Hill
Kraken Cove
N
E
S
W
Welcomes All

First Street Shops & Creatures

BUILDING NAME: THE BANDAGED HEART
BUILDING TYPE: CLINIC
ADDRESS: 1 FIRST STREET

STAFF:
DOCTOR: CALLA KNAGGS
SPECIES: GOBLIN
NURSE: TILLY WILLIAMS
SPECIES: HUMAN
SECRETARY: KATIE FLUTURE
SPECIES: MONARCH FAIRY

BUILDING NAME: THE SPARKLING CAULDRON
BUILDING TYPE: APOTHECARY
ADDRESS: 2 FIRST STREET

STAFF:
APOTHERCARY: SAMARA HICKEY
SPECIES: NAGA

BUILDING NAME: THE WINGED APPLE
BUILDING TYPE: GENERAL STORE
ADDRESS: 3 FIRST STREET

STAFF:
OWNER: PIERRE AUDET
SPECIES: GARGOYLE

BUILDING NAME: THE FLOWERING TEAPOT
BUILDING TYPE: CAFÉ AND BAKERY
ADDRESS: 4 FIRST STREET

STAFF:
OWNER: ANNAMAE HONEYCUTT
SPECIES: DRYAD
OWNER: RICHARD HONEYCUTT
SPECIES: HUMAN

Second Street Shops & Creatures

BUILDING NAME: THE HORNED PEARL
BUILDING TYPE: SCALES, NAILS, & HORN CARE
ADDRESS: 5 SECOND STREET

STAFF:
OWNER: CALIXTA TERRAL
SPECIES: SUCCUBUS

BUILDING NAME: THE VINY SHEARS
BUILDING TYPE: BARBERSHOP & HAIR SALON
ADDRESS: 6 SECOND STREET

STAFF:
OWNER: BERYL TERRAL
SPECIES: ORC

BUILDING NAME: THE CROWNED BOOT
BUILDING TYPE: CLOTHING & FABRIC STORE
ADDRESS: 7 SECOND STREET

STAFF:
OWNER: PEREGRINE FERNSBY
SPECIES: SATYR

Third Street Shops & Creatures

BUILDING NAME: THE LONELY RAKE
BUILDING TYPE: HARDWARE & GARDEN SUPPLIES
ADDRESS: 8 THIRD STREET

STAFF:
OWNER: AURELIUS GLYDENBOLLOCKS
SPECIES: MOTHMAN

BUILDING NAME: THE DANCING DAISY
BUILDING TYPE: BOOKS & STATIONERY STORE
ADDRESS: 9 THIRD STREET

STAFF:
OWNER: LUCILLE HOLMES
SPECIES: HUMAN

BUILDING NAME: THE SINGING SEAHORSE
BUILDING TYPE: PUB & KARAOKE BAR
ADDRESS: 10 THIRD STREET

STAFF:
OWNER: MARISOL AZZARA
SPECIES: SIREN

Beck

Prologue

Invigorated by my swim, I shift into my human form as I pull myself out of the ocean and onto the dock, then check my watch sitting on top of my folded clothing to make sure I'm still on time.

Thankfully I'm ahead of schedule, my dragon not demanding too much attention from me this morning, leaving me free to fulfill all my duties as guardian of Starry Hill—including being the island's ferryman and errand runner in the city, as required by today's agenda.

That was a really good swim, I tell my dragon. *Next time, let's see if we can go even faster.*

I quickly dry myself with my water magic before pulling on my pants and shirt, then hop in my boat and set off for Cape Easton while my dragon falls into a contented slumber within my chest.

As I lower my hand into the water to guide the boat along the current, I focus on the supplies I need to pick up for Marisol as she prepares for another ladies' night at The Singing Seahorse. Going through the very specific list of everything she needs for their themed cocktails helps to distract me from another item on my timetable—a name, one that reminds of someone I knew a long time ago.

A friend. Best friend.

Eleanor. Or Nori as I used to call her.

But I know I'm not lucky enough to entertain any hope that it could actually be her. Fate has never been that kind to me.

I push away the fond yet painful memories from the last day I saw Nori, and focus on everything else that needs to happen before I ferry the commercial lawyer to our island so she can help Maisie with her new cakery.

Guiding my boat toward the familiar slot at Cape Easton harbor reserved for Starry Hill, I call on my dragon to help me scan for any threats. He opens a sleepy eye and halfheartedly scents the air. Satisfied it's safe as usual, my dragon goes back to sleep and I make quick work of securing the boat before heading into the city's streets to pick up all the orders.

I'm done much earlier than anticipated, jitters I'm not accustomed to holding my mind and my body captive all day, forcing me to return to the dock and wait for the stranger. I'm not even able to slip into my favorite gaming store to check if their new dice boxes have arrived.

Ignoring my desire to pace up and down, I root my feet to the dock while I monitor the hands on the watch nearing one o'clock, wondering if she'll be late. Usually creatures are respectful of departure times, but I've had a couple of situations where we've been severely delayed due to their tardiness, which affects the entirety of my schedule for the rest of the day. Though, I do make an effort to remain polite regardless.

I'm still looking down as I sense someone approaching behind me, my dragon raising his head with renewed vigor as their fresh floral scent drifts downwind.

The moment I turn around, every other thought ceases to exist as my whole world realigns and my breath catches in my throat.

It's my Nori.

She looks completely different, grown up, but I'd recognize her anywhere. Hair still the shade of a copper penny glinting in the sun, pulled back and constrained in a sleek bun, and familiar honey-brown eyes that hold so much warmth, even when tinged with nerves.

Nori's so beautiful it sends my heart into a full-speed sprint. There aren't sufficient words in my brain to explain how good it is to see her again, so I remain silent as I stare at her.

"Beck?" Nori asks carefully, her gaze heavy as she assesses me. It's obvious she doesn't recognize me, and I try not to let that hurt my feelings. I mean, why would she after all these years?

"Eleanor?" I return with a slight bow, keeping my tone polite and professional like I'd use with any newcomer I have to ferry to Starry Hill.

Eyes widening, Nori sucks in a breath. After a beat, she whispers tentatively, "Shinsu?"

Hearing her say my real name, one I haven't used in twenty-two years, sends a thrill careening through my body. Memories of happy, carefree days together, of sunshine and laughter hitting me all at once.

My dragon sits tall, almost wagging his tail, and despite trying to suppress him out here in public, sends scales flashing across my cheeks and neck, hoping to get her attention.

Needing to fully confirm it truly is my former best friend, I manage to utter, "Nori?"

Nori's lips lift at the corners as she approaches me. "How long has it been? Last time I saw you, you were—"

"We were twelve. It's been twenty-two years," I say, still stuck to the same spot as I try to process that this stunning woman really is my Nori, and I might actually have her back in my life again.

"Wait. You remember?" Nori asks, hope ringing in her voice as she pauses a couple of steps away from me.

"I've never forgotten you," I answer honestly, not adequately able to express how often I've thought about that last day I saw her and how drastically my life changed after that.

We remain frozen for a few more seconds, and I can't think of where to start with everything I want to ask her, all I want to know about her.

Should I start by apologizing for leaving without saying goodbye? But if I do, then she'll ask me where I went and I'm not ready to get into that. Do I ask her when she came to the city? But what if she asks me the same question? What do I say then?

Can I tell her how beautiful she is? Dare I ask her to be friends again?

In the end, I say nothing. I simply point toward the boat and when she hesitates to get in, I offer her my hand.

Nori's palms are soft and clammy. I wrinkle my nose as I detect some nerves present in her scent, and wonder if I should ask if it's about me, or my boat. But Tilly has taught me it's impolite to comment on someone's scent so maybe it's better to wait for Nori to speak first once she feels comfortable. Don't lawyers like talking anyway?

When I place my hand in the water, a bit of tension seeps out of my shoulders and my dragon luxuriates in our connection to the ocean. He stays present for the entirety of the quiet trip, staring at Nori, sending scales fluttering down various parts of my body whenever we detect her eyes on us.

In the distance, I spot Ren and Maisie waiting on the Starry Hill dock and point them out to Nori. "The incubus is Ren, and the human waving excitedly is Maisie."

Nori grins. "It's nice to put faces to their names. Or it will be once we get closer and I can see them properly."

I cringe at having forgotten she might not be able to see as clearly as I can, and my dragon retreats with a huff. "Ah yes. Human eyes don't always see that well. I apologize."

"Oh no. That's not anything to apologize for. I didn't mean—" Nori cuts herself off by pressing her lips together, a bright red blush spreading across her cheeks as she stares at her lap.

As we near, Maisie bounces on her toes, one arm waving profusely while the other remains locked around Ren's. I slow the boat down, guiding us into my spot at the dock, and Ren grabs the rope I toss toward him and secures it to a cleat.

"Eleanor! Welcome to Starry Hill. Thank you so much for coming out here to meet us and to help me set up The Tangerine Grove Cakery," Maisie says as she takes both of Nori's hands in hers then pulls her into a hug.

I frown at them, because never did it even cross my mind that it's possible to simply hug someone you've just met. Should I have tried to hug Nori earlier? Would that have made it easier for her to talk to me?

Ren removes his hand from his hoodie pocket and holds it out for Nori. "Hi. I'm Ren. And that's my Maisie. We really do appreciate you coming out here and for all the work you've put into helping us set up Maisie's cakery."

Pride seeps into me at how easily Ren talks to Nori, at how much he's grown since he's been with Maisie and how he's managing his social anxiety. Not too long ago he was stuck in his house, hardly having the courage to leave it for short trips, and now he's having conversations with strangers.

A tiny fantasy enters my head, of the four of us together on some kind of double date, but I quickly squash it. I'm not even able to have a simple dialogue with Nori, so how could I entertain any romantic thoughts. Having her shoot me down would hurt more than the first time I lost her.

Nori shakes Ren's hand. "I'm Eleanor. And it really is my pleasure to be here. Any excuse to get out of the office is a good one, but coming to Starry Hill is just so much better."

Hearing her say her full name reminds me that she's actually Eleanor, not Nori, and certainly not *my* Nori. Calling her anything but Eleanor will probably not be polite.

Maisie hooks her arm through Eleanor's. "Can we show you around the town later? We'll head to the cottage first so you can see what we've done so far, because that's actually why you came, right? Can't have a business be official if I don't have all the right paperwork, but afterward I can take you to The Flowering Teapot, or The Winged Apple, or The Crowned Boot. Any of the shops on the hill would be perfect for your first visit."

Eleanor opens her mouth to respond, glancing at me almost as if she wants me to give her advice. Can I ask her to visit me too? Maybe I can point out where I live and she can stop by for lemonade before I take her back to Cape Easton? Or if I know what time they're going to The Flowering Teapot then I can happen to be there at the same time.

Before I'm able to decide what to suggest, Ren says gently, "Let's get everything done with the cakery first and then we can see what Eleanor feels up for when we're finished."

Eleanor offers everyone a small smile. "Sounds like a plan," she says as she walks away with Ren and Maisie, and I remain frozen to the dock.

I don't see her again for the rest of the afternoon, and the boat ride back to Cape Easton that evening is just as quiet as the first one.

When we dock at the harbor, Eleanor gives me a small piece of paper. "This is my number."

I stare down at her handwriting and her full name written in cursive, nostalgia raking down my back at how different it looks compared to the way she used to sign my notes. "Thank you."

Eleanor swallows hard and clutches her big bag closer to her. "It was nice to see you again."

I nod, a wistful smile pulling on my lips. "It was. Quite a surprise. But nice."

"Yes. A big surprise," Eleanor echoes before our conversation tapers back into awkward silence.

"Do you have a car?" I ask, looking toward the darkening lot.

"Yes. I didn't park far."

"Good."

After another quiet stretch that lasts about three seconds but feels like three minutes, Eleanor says, "I guess I'll see you around."

"That'll be nice," I answer, hoping it to really be true.

I stay put and watch Eleanor as she carefully makes her way toward her car, waiting for her to drive off before I finally let my shoulders slump. My dragon crawls deeper into my chest, giving me his back, just as disappointed in me as I am.

If I ever get the opportunity to see Eleanor again, I hope I'll be able to do better than today. She deserves a proper explanation for why I disappeared, even if it hurts me to dredge up old memories.

CHAPTER 1

I pull at the neckline of my baby blue blouse, adjusting my ample boobs resting on top of their underwire support to resemble something perky. Tonight, I have liberated my assets from the confines of high-necked boxy work blouses and embraced every single feminine curve of mine with this sweetheart neckline.

Not quite sure if I'll get used to seeing so much of myself when I look down, but it was nice for a change to enjoy getting ready and putting on something cute.

Working in a male-dominated field, I constantly strive to blend in, hiding any hints of myself that could remind them that

I'm a woman. Each boxy shirt I don helps me chameleon myself, activating my lawyer side where I can pretend to be just as tough as them.

But tonight, I get to simply be me—a girls' girl who's actually a sensitive softy and who gets overstimulated easily.

When I go to adjust my shirt again, Audrey swats at my hand, an echo to my inner voice.

"Stop fussing. Your tits look amazing. *You* look amazing," she emphasizes, hooking her arm through mine, effectively stilling my incessant clothing adjustments as she leads me away from her parked car and toward Cape Easton's harbor. More specifically, the farthest dock reserved for boats going to Starry Hill, our destination today.

I've only been to their dock once before, but not a day has passed that I haven't thought about it, and Shinsu—or Beck, as he prefers to go by now. Unexpectedly seeing him after twenty-two years completely caught me off guard, and we both found ourselves fumbling for words. Who I remember as a lanky preteen boy has turned into a statuesque male with a sharp jawline and wide-set shoulders that have kept my late-night thoughts occupied more times than I care to admit. And those pale eyes of his and the way they raked over me when he realized who I was, they may have featured in a couple of naughty fantasies a time or two. Or three.

Almost obsessively, I've replayed our interactions from that day, rewriting them again and again, each one vastly better than the awkward reality that it was. I may even have practiced what I would say if we were to run into each other again. Like tonight, perhaps. Because finding out someone you haven't seen since you were twelve is a dragon and *the* guardian of Starry Hill, it does make one a little curious. Okay, more than curious. I have so many questions and I didn't get to ask any of them last time. I just hope my courage doesn't fail me again.

Wrenching my thoughts back to the present, I bump my shoulder playfully against Audrey's. "Thank you, bestest neighbor in all the land. It's been a while since I've had this much boobage on display, but tonight seemed like the perfect opportunity to try something different, something that feels more like the real me." *And it has nothing to do with Beck or trying to show him I'm not a kid anymore,* I add silently, futilely trying to convince myself.

"I'm glad you did. You're doing yourself and the entire population of the world interested, and not interested, in titties a disservice by not having those bad boys out for our viewing pleasure."

The cackle that escapes me is abrupt and loud and I quickly clamp a hand over my mouth to contain it, though some muffled giggles still manage to break free. "Why, thank you, my dear," I say with an affected accent, flipping some of my long ginger hair over my shoulder.

I've always loved the rich copper of my hair, a "crown of fire" Beck called it once when we were nine and playing outside, but I've yet to embrace my natural curls. Perhaps one day I'd be comfortable enough to set them free. Baby steps.

Audrey and I stroll toward the end of the dock, my gaze jumping over each boat moored in place before settling on an unfamiliar boat waiting in the spot that Beck's was in last time. I try to be inconspicuous about it, but my eyes quickly scan the waters of Indigo Bay beyond the harbor, just in case he's on his way and I might have missed him.

Audrey gives me a sideward glance, likely reading something in my expression that isn't there. Not anything I'd like to acknowledge anyway.

Propping her hands on her slim hips, Audrey raises a brow and drawls, "So, I know we're going for a ladies' night, but you haven't said much about your previous visit to Starry Hill. Any cuties catch your eye?"

My cheeks instantly heat as Beck's face flashes behind my eyes, the smattering of shimmery scales on his cheeks and down his neck printed into my brain. He definitely didn't have those before. Just last night I imagined what they would feel like if I were to trace them with my fingers, if they would be hard or smooth to the touch. But that is a thought that I'll never voice nor dream to actually experience in reality.

"Oh, uhm," I start, suddenly finding my tongue tied and clumsy. If my mother saw me stumbling over my words like this she would question if I actually am a good lawyer. Thank goodness I went into commercial law and not into prosecution like she originally wanted me to do. Though, dragging myself out of bed to go to the office every day is becoming harder and harder with each year that passes in my oppressive company.

"Why, Eleanor, is that a blush I see?" Audrey teases, poking my arm playfully as she wiggles her eyebrows up and down.

"Ooo! Who's blushing and why?" a purple-haired woman asks excitedly as she comes skipping down the dock, her seashell bangles clinking together rhythmically. What can only be described as a completely infatuated and devoted partner follows closely behind her, monitoring her every move as if she's a goddess and he her humble servant.

"Juniper!" Audrey calls, wrapping the newcomer in a hug. "This is our blushing Eleanor, whom I've managed to drag out of her miserable little apartment to join us for ladies' night at The Singing Seahorse." Reading the confused frown on my face, Audrey quickly adds, "I get to call it miserable because our units are exactly the same, and mine has been pretty lonely since Tilly moved out, so I'm choosing to believe yours is just as dreary. And a fun time with the gals, and perhaps some eye candy along the way, sounds like a much better way to spend a Saturday night."

"I wouldn't go as far as calling it miserable, but it certainly fails to be as exciting as everything you and Maisie have told me I can expect tonight." If Audrey hadn't invited me along, I would've crawled into my plush reading chair with one of my well-loved historical romances and been swept away into a land of dashing gentlemen pining for their ladies. It's one of my favorite ways to escape reality and de-stress after a grueling day at work, but I didn't want to miss another opportunity to visit charming Starry Hill again. Or see Beck.

"Wait. Are you *the* Eleanor? The fancy lawyer who's helping Maisie set up her business?"

"Oh, uhm, yes. That would be me," I say, with an awkward wave, my blush deepening at her knowing who I am and me not having a clue who they are.

"Maisie and Ren have been singing your praises about how much you've helped with preparing her cakery," she practically gushes, the warmth in her tone making my shoulders relax. "I'm sorry, I'm Juniper and this is my lovely Viggo. He's my kraken boyfriend."

Juniper pulls Viggo forward and I try my best to keep my eyes on his face and not scan for any signs of tentacles as I stretch out my hand for him to shake. Even though it's becoming more normal to see creatures of all kinds around Cape Easton, I haven't met a kraken before, and I don't want to inadvertently do something that would be considered rude.

Strong fingers wrap around mine and Viggo's mouth pulls into a kind grin as he throws his free arm around Juniper, pulling her back to his front. "Nice to meet you, Eleanor. I'll be taking you lovely ladies to Starry Hill tonight."

"Not Beck?" I catch myself too late and mortification flutters cold fingers down my spine. My eyes round and Viggo's brows pull together, a question lying in wait while a smirk of curiosity dances around Juniper's mouth.

Saving me from having to explain myself, Viggo teases lightly, "Sorry, you're stuck with me on this trip. I've been trying to help out more with ferrying visitors across from the city and take a bit off Beck's very full plate."

Juniper laces her fingers with Viggo's hand draped over her shoulder as she gives him a coy smile. "Well, it also helps that my thrift shop is here and Viggo wants me to stay with him in the evenings."

Lowering his face to Juniper's ear, Viggo's voice drops to a deep purr. "Don't pretend you don't like being wrapped in my tentacles all night."

My cheeks heat anew as I imagine all the places tentacles can explore. Before I can catch myself, my mind wanders toward male dragon anatomy and the unconfirmed claims I've read online of how much they differ from humans. I've spent quite a bit of time looking for any references or information about water dragons, but wasn't able to find much. From what I can gather, they're fairly secretive and keep to themselves, which only makes me even more curious about Beck.

Audrey hooks a thumb toward me. "Let's not scar Eleanor with your tentacle sex talk. Yet. At least buy the girl a drink first."

My mouth gapes open. *Am I about to be propositioned for a threesome? An orgy?*

Apparently reading the shock, confusion, and near panic on my face, Juniper quickly adds, "We're monogamous. Don't worry. But I am guilty of oversharing. If you have any questions about creature features, I'm your girl."

"Oh, okay," I say on a relieved exhale. "I might take you up on that offer. After a drink, or two."

Audrey nods enthusiastically. "Me too. I have questions. Many, many questions."

Juniper's laugh is effervescent as she hops into the boat. "I'm sure you do."

Viggo helps Audrey in, then offers his hand for me as I hesitate on the dock, my eyes roaming over the narrow hull, my feet not quite ready to leave the safety of the land. It's not exactly that I'm scared of the ocean, but I'm also not *not* scared of it. I just hold a certain level of profound respect for its mysterious depths and the diverse, and somewhat terrifying, creatures living beneath the surface.

"How do you know Beck?" Viggo asks brightly, his hand still outstretched.

Appreciating his attempt at redirecting my attention, I place my hand in his and step into the boat where Juniper quickly takes my other hand and gently pulls me down to sit snuggly between her and Audrey.

I give them a subtle yet very grateful nod at their smooth coordinating assistance and tap into my lawyer side, suppressing any emotions to lay out the simple facts. "Beck's grandmother lived next door to us when I was small. He came to visit her every summer and we'd be inseparable from sunrise to sunset. Then, one morning, in the middle of summer, he was just gone. I went to check with his grandmother if he was okay, but she simply said he had left, gone home early, without any further explanation. I never saw him again. Until a few months ago when he was waiting right here on the dock."

"Ooo. So you guys go way back. Did he explain what happened?" Juniper asks eagerly, leaning forward as she squeezes my hand.

I shake my head, a little bit of disappointment bleeding into my voice. "Nope. We both recognized each other, acknowledged that it's been over two decades since we've seen each other, then..."

"Then?" Viggo asks, apparently also engrossed in my sad tale.

I shrug. "Then we rode in silence the rest of the way."

Juniper winces. "Oh. That's..."

"Awkward," Audrey says with a grimace.

"Sweet," Viggo corrects with a knowing tilt to his chin.

My head swivels between the three of them. "Huh?"

Viggo taps his finger against his temple. "You were both nervous and got stuck in your smarty-pants heads, probably overthinking everything, and ended up saying nothing."

"You think?" Now that he mentions it, it definitely felt like that for me. I kept thinking about what to ask Beck and obsessing over how to word it perfectly, that I kind of froze and ended up saying nothing. Would Beck have felt a similar pressure to say the exact right thing to me, too?

"Yeah," Juniper encourages, her bright blue eyes kind as she squeezes my hand. "Maybe ask him when you can see him again?"

My refusal is quick, the little bit of courage I felt left on the dock in Cape Easton. "I wouldn't want to bother him."

From his spot at the helm, Viggo bounces on his toes, his eyes twinkling with excitement as he guides us out of the harbor. "Oh, it won't be a bother, believe me. A woman like *you* giving *him* attention, he'd be rolling over and asking for belly pats if given the chance."

The thought seems preposterous to me, but I decide not to voice it. Despite my clear attraction to Beck, I'm under no false pretenses that someone as cool as him would be interested in me. They also don't need to know that I gave him my number when he took me back to Cape Easton, nor that he never called me. My pride can't handle that level of embarrassment.

Though, if I do have the opportunity to see Beck again, I'm going to try my best to talk to him. I want to know why he disappeared all those years ago and never even bothered to say goodbye. And if I'm feeling extra brave, I might even ask why he didn't call me this time. Having answers would be so much better than being stuck in this unknown I've been in for so long. I can always nurse my wounded feelings later.

After all, there is the possibility that we might have gotten our wires crossed last time, and perhaps there was some miscommunication. And maybe, just maybe, we can try to be friends again.

CHAPTER 2

The aroma of freshly baked bread fills my kitchen as I open the oven to take my focaccia out. Carefully placing the bread on a wire rack to cool, I sneak a quick peek out my cottage's window before grabbing some supplies from the fridge to start on the charcuterie board for our boys' game night.

My old stone mill cottage is strategically located on the northern edge of the island, giving me a clear view of anyone approaching from the mainland. It would take me less than two seconds to dive into the ocean and shift into my dragon form to protect Starry Hill from any threats, though that has never been needed in the fourteen years I've called this island home.

Hands filled with all the snacks I got from The Winged Apple—per Pierre's suggestion as well as numerous hours of research—I pause in front of the window for the umpteenth time, my eyes raking over the dark blue water in the distance, my ears straining for any familiar sounds of Viggo's boat.

"Why do you keep looking out the window?" Ren asks, taking up position next to me as he also rakes his gaze over the same patch of ocean.

It's been three months since I saw Nori—Eleanor—in Cape Easton harbor, but I've thought about her every single day since.

Eleanor has always been pretty, but the woman who stood in front of me that day was breathtakingly beautiful. She has a body sculpted by the gods, voluptuous feminine curves hiding underneath formal office wear. At night when I'm alone in bed, I like to imagine what she really looks like underneath it all, wondering if her skin would feel as soft as it looks under my exploring fingers and worshipful mouth.

But I'm still angry at myself for how poorly I handled our meeting, my dragon sharing the sentiment by remaining quiet, withdrawn, except for when we swim in my shifted form.

That day, my brain filled with a million things I wanted to tell her, but the more thoughts entered my mind, the less I was able to verbalize them, the words getting jumbled in my throat, each thought competing for dominance, until all I could offer her was my fraught silence.

Placing the supplies on the counter, I organize them by importance while I search for an explanation to give Ren, wanting to stay as close to the truth as possible without being completely transparent. "I'm looking out for Viggo. He should be arriving anytime soon. He's bringing Audrey and Eleanor with him and Juniper," I state factually, feeling a little proud of myself at the smooth cover.

Ren leans against my counter, propping one hand behind him as he watches me with a curious gaze, his long red tail resting against his leg. "Maisie mentioned Eleanor is coming. She's been incredibly helpful with getting all the paperwork for the cakery aboveboard."

My entire body stills as I glance at Ren. "Are Maisie and Eleanor friends?"

Ren's brows draw together and he quirks his head to the side. "I think so. Why?"

"Would Eleanor come visit Maisie after she doesn't need her help anymore?" I ask flatly, not wanting them to take advantage of her and discard her when she's no longer useful to them.

"I hope so, yes," Ren answers carefully, studying my face keenly as he straightens up. "I mean, the ladies invited her tonight and that has nothing to do with work." Before I can throw out another question, Ren's mouth tilts into a tender grin that's reserved for anything to do with Maisie. "And you know my Maisie. She's already compiled a list of everything she wants to make for Eleanor. Besides, the treats she made for The Singing Seahorse tonight were inspired by Eleanor's favorite flavors."

Relief seeps through my bones on a tangible wave, my dragon sending scales flickering in their wake down my spine, as a small smile perches on my lips. "Yeah, what cake does she like?"

Ren pops his hands into his hoodie's pockets and arches a brow. "Why do you want to know?"

"I—"

"You?" Ren prods gently.

"I just want you guys to be nice to her," I explain lamely, focusing my attention back on the charcuterie board in the hopes that the inquisition ends there.

Ren straightens up, his eyes widening as he stares at me. "Wait. How do you know Eleanor?"

"Bodin is here," I sputter, turning on my heel and heading to the door to welcome my second guest to arrive.

I'm not quite sure how much I want to tell anyone about Eleanor, I hardly speak about my time before Starry Hill, but I grab the excuse to pivot away from the conversation like it's a lifeline thrown by fate herself.

Nearly a head taller than me, my orc friend fills the door, his smile warm as he clasps my shoulder in a friendly greeting. "Beck, so kind of you to host our first game night. I brought some Berserker Brown Ale for us to enjoy," Bodin says, gesturing to the oak keg under his arm.

"It is my pleasure," I say as I usher him inside, one eye still trained on the window on the opposite wall. "And thank you for bringing the beer. I've prepared some bread and light snacks. Ren brought tangerines and some kind of cake that Maisie made." Guilt claws at me for condensing Maisie's incredible baking skills to such a poor explanation, but my mind is still preoccupied by Eleanor's imminent arrival.

Bodin clasps Ren's hand and pulls him into a hug before placing the keg in the kitchen. "I spoke to Arran earlier. He said he'll be here after sundown. He's running low on vampire sunscreen and wants to save what he has for a 'special occasion,' even though Tilly told him that she's ordered more."

Feeling that the focaccia has cooled enough, I place it on my wooden cutting board as I say over my shoulder, "Arran's always been mindful with how he spends money, so it makes sense for him to time his excursions when it's least burdensome to him or others."

There's a small pause before Bodin remarks, "That's very observant of you, Beck."

"Here comes Viggo," Ren says, pointing out the window facing the ocean.

I force my feet to stay put, casually lifting my head to peer over Ren's shoulder. Bodin flanks Ren, effectively blocking my view, before I reluctantly join them so I can also watch Viggo steer his boat toward the dock, instantly spotting Eleanor's bright hair among the others.

My heart pounds a rapid staccato in my chest and I force long, slow breaths through my nose in an effort to disguise the nerves coursing through my body, feeling woefully underprepared to see Eleanor again after she's occupied most of my thoughts for months.

"Is that Eleanor with Juniper and Audrey?" Bodin asks.

"Yes." My voice is even. Controlled. Unaffected.

"She's pretty," Bodin says, stating the obvious.

"You're married," I remind him, my dragon now fully awake and narrowing his eyes at Bodin.

Ren shifts his focus away from the window and turns toward me. "Do you know Eleanor, or did she just make that much of an impression on you? It seems like there's something more there than a simple ride to the island." There's a depth of compassion in his tone as he tries to coax a real answer from me, effectively lowering my walls.

Feeling safe between my friends, I stare longingly at Eleanor as she disembarks, her long vibrant hair dancing with little flames from the rays of the setting sun behind her. "Growing up, she was my best friend, my absolute favorite person. But we were children then, and I've not seen her until that day I brought her here for Maisie."

"Go talk to her!" Ren encourages, excitement trickling into his voice.

"I'm scared," I admit softly, admiring how beautiful she looks in a soft blue shirt that highlights her best features. She's even more stunning than the images I conjured in my head late at night.

"Of what?" Bodin asks, laying a hand on my shoulder. "You'll never know anything unless you try."

"I'm scared we've changed too much since then and maybe she wouldn't like who I am now." *Or maybe she won't forgive me for how I left*, I add silently.

"Bullshit," Bodin says with a laugh. "Never assume anything. Pull on your big boy pants and go have a conversation with her. But first, let her go enjoy her time with the girls while we get some liquid courage in you."

"Okay. I can do that." I don't know if I'm convincing them or myself, but my dragon echoes the sentiment, both of us adamant to at least try this time.

CHAPTER 3

The Singing Seahorse is absolutely charming. The dark wood floors and mahogany furniture, the sconces dotted along the old stone walls, and the feminine touch with its coral accents and deep azure fabrics make it the prettiest pub I've seen in my life.

Everything about tonight, about this place, has exceeded every single one of my expectations.

Each creature I've met has been lovely, welcoming me into their fold like a long-lost friend. I've received genuine compliments for my outfit and even my hair, but most significantly, many have gushed about the work I've put into helping Maisie with her cakery. The heartfelt interest in each other's lives is such a stark contrast to what I'm used to, and a not-so-tiny part of me longs to have more of this community in my life.

Tonight I've been able to simply be myself. Not an ounce of self-consciousness has entered my body as I've chatted to new friends while enjoying some delectable treats or while letting loose on the dance floor. I've danced so much that even my meticulously straightened hair has gone frizzy. Here, there's no need to care about anything superficial. We can revel in being unfiltered versions of ourselves.

Catching Audrey's arm once she's finished a rather impressive twirl, I pull her toward me and raise my voice to be heard above the music. "I'm going to get some water and sit down a bit. Be back soon."

"Okey dokey," Audrey sing-songs before planting a kiss on my cheek. She raises her arms above her head and meanders toward the front of the dance floor, where she joins Maisie and Calixta in some vigorously suggestive moves that should come with a parental advisory notice.

Giggling to myself, I grab a glass of water from the bar counter and a carrot cupcake before slinking toward the back of the room where the music is at a more manageable volume. I flop into a booth and sigh contentedly as my overstimulated self takes a quiet moment to breathe in all the joy in the air.

"I know that look," an elderly human lady says as she lowers herself down next to me. "It's the 'I'm having so much fun, but I need a break from the noise, but I also don't want to be too far from the action either' look."

My cheeks burn as I wince. "Is it that obvious?"

"Well, it takes one to know one," she says with a quick wink, the kindness in her eyes making my short-lived tension seep out of my shoulders.

"Glad to know I'm in good company." My smile is wide as I hold out my hand for her. "I'm Eleanor."

"I know who you are, dear. It's very, very nice to officially meet you. I'm Lucille. I'm the owner of the shop next door: The Dancing Daisy."

Not surprised that she recognizes me since I'm the only newcomer tonight, I skip over the cryptic comment and choose to focus on her shop. "I adore all the business names on Starry Hill. What kind of goods do you have at The Dancing Daisy?"

"It's a bookshop. We also have stationery and a small candy section that's well frequented by the town." Just by the warmth in her voice when talking about The Dancing Daisy, I know how much she loves her shop.

Turning in my seat to face her more directly, I place a hand on my heart as I say, "Lucille, you just named all of my favorite things in the entire world. I think we're meant to be friends."

The lines around Lucille's eyes deepen as she grins. "Would you like to come see it? I'd love to have you over for some tea, then we can compare notes on our favorite books."

I'm already nodding before she's finished talking. "You name the time, and I'll be there."

"How's next weekend?"

"It's a date."

"Who's got a date?" Doc Calla asks as she hops onto the bench next to Lucille. The goblin doctor might be small in stature, but I've quickly learned that she balances that with her wit and tenderheartedness. Not only did she adopt Bodin and his twin sister Beryl when they arrived on Starry Hill as young kids, but from what Audrey and Tilly have told me, she's also the town's de facto matriarch.

"We do," Lucille answers, laying her parchmenty hand on mine. "Dear Eleanor is going to come visit my shop next weekend for some tea and book talk."

Something passes between the two older women before Doc Calla turns her intelligent hazel eyes on me. "Welcome to Starry Hill, Eleanor. We hope you'll be very happy with each second you spend here."

My mouth opens and closes a couple of times while I try to make sense of her comment. I'm just visiting, but it almost sounds like she's welcoming me as a resident. That's not happening. It's not like they need commercial lawyers here very often.

Choosing not to correct Doc Calla, I smile and thank her. "I've had a lot of fun tonight, and I hope there are many more events like this to come. Thank you for allowing me to join."

Lucille pats my hand. "Talking about fun, it's about time us old ladies head back home before things get really rowdy."

Doc Calla cocks a brow at her friend. "Don't pretend you don't like all the rowdiness."

"Oh, you know I do. But I've reached my limit for today." Turning back to me, Lucille asks, "Eleanor, are you staying on the island tonight or heading home?"

I lift my chin to quickly scan the crowd. "Audrey and I are heading back tonight. Viggo offered to take us, but I'm not sure when. Come to think of it, I haven't seen Juniper for some time either."

Doc Calla's mouth lifts into a knowing smirk. "Viggo snuck Juniper away quite a while ago, but I'm sure they'll resurface soon." It takes me a moment to realize she means that quite literally—Viggo probably has Juniper somewhere in the ocean, doing some fun stuff with his tentacles to her.

Before I can think of an appropriate response, Lucille suggests, "Or, you can ask Beck to take you."

At the mention of his name, heat spreads down my face and over my chest. "I wouldn't want to impose," I say quickly, not wanting Beck to see me sweaty and unkempt like this.

Doc Calla leans back in her seat as she studies me, patience and wisdom reflecting in her eyes as a gentle sliver of a smile pulls at her mouth. "Please do. I'm very certain that dragon wouldn't mind some imposing from you."

"Oh?" I squeak, my gaze ricocheting off every surface as my brain scrambles to decipher what she means. I might be a grown woman at thirty-four, but it seems that even the mere mention of Beck takes me back to my awkward preteen self and the innocent little crush I had on him back then. The little crush that might be repeating itself now.

Lucille shoos her friend out of the booth. "I'm afraid we've said too much. Just be gentle with him," she says, scooting along toward the edge of the bench. Pausing, she adds, "But not too gentle. Perhaps a good conversation is needed. Direct honesty goes a long way with him."

A little confused, I stare at the two ladies now standing on the other side of the table. "I'll try to remember that if I run into him again."

Doc Calla wiggles her eyebrows at me, and before walking out of the pub, says, "I'm certain you will."

BECK

CHAPTER 4

My gaze flits around the table, my heart feeling fuller with each burst of rumbustious laughter from my friends as they discuss their characters while snacking on foods I prepared.

For so long, I've felt lonely, but something has shifted in Starry Hill over the last year or so, and even if Arran and I have not found life partners like Bodin and Ren have, there's a wholeness in our community, and in particular, in this friendship—this brotherhood—that eases that ache of loneliness.

Arran leans back in his seat and runs a hand over his cropped reddish-brown hair. The shade reminds me of Eleanor's, but it's nowhere near as vibrant or lustrous as hers.

"This has certainly turned into more fun of an evening than I could have predicted," the vampire states with almost a question hovering at the end of the sentence.

My brows dip into a frown as I try to decipher the meaning of the statement while awaiting confirmation from the other two that they, too, are equally surprised by the level of fun they've had in my home.

Ren lazes back and slips his hands in his hoodie pockets as he shoots me a reassuring smile. "I agree. I've always wanted to try playing Knights and Castles but I honestly didn't think anyone else would be into it."

Bodin nods and pats me on the shoulder in what I would consider an affectionate way. "If it weren't for you, I wouldn't even know this game existed. And while we're being honest, if you were to explain it to me in any other setting, I don't think I would've given it a shot. Thank you, Beck."

My chest swells with pride and I can't even attempt to fight the smile quirking at my lips as I dip my head in acknowledgment of their praise.

Arran drains his beer and lowers the glass with a thunk on the table. "We are in agreement there too, young orc. Never did I think I'd find so much enjoyment in designing my own character and determining his ability scores in a make-believe world."

I refill Arran's glass and raise my own to his. "It really means so much to me to have you here, all three of you, and that you appreciate the quests and adventures we'll go on. As Game Master, I promise to do my utmost best to design the most adventurous campaign for our knights."

Ren and Bodin join their glasses to ours in a hearty salute, and that inexplicable bubble of happiness in my chest gets even bigger.

Throughout the evening, all three of my guests have enjoyed their beer along with their snacks, getting more relaxed with each passing hour. I, however, have been nursing the same glass since they arrived, too preoccupied with explaining the game and not wanting my brain to be clouded by alcohol. I may have also positioned myself with a perfect view of the darkened dock beyond my window, keeping an eye out for Eleanor.

My dragon lifts his snout and sniffs the air, also keeping a surreptitious lookout for any trace of Eleanor's lavender scent. Despite still being annoyed with me, he's not gone back to sleep since she's set foot on the island.

I'm going to try to do better this time, I promise him and myself, both of us eager to right my wrongs.

Ren draws my attention back to the table with a certain glint in his eye, his gaze also flicking to the window for a second as if he knows exactly where my mind has gone. "Where did you learn to play Knights and Castles?"

Thankful not to expose the obvious direction of my thoughts, I dip my chin at Ren. "In boarding school," I say, rolling a d20 die between my fingers. "We were in a pretty isolated location, more so than Starry Hill. Some students chose to sneak off into the forest and get up to mischief in our free time, but a few of us preferred to get lost in worlds where we didn't have to be the scary creatures everyone feared, but rather knights on quests to save our realm."

Bodin elbows me a little sloppily. "Or a pretty damsel, or two."

An image of holding Eleanor in my armored arms after saving her from some awful calamity fills my mind. "There was definitely some of that thought too."

Arran palms the table and stares intently at us. "When can we meet again? Surely we aren't doing this once a month when the females have their scheduled events? I have plans for my knight."

"Can we meet weekly?" Ren asks.

I aim for my nod not to look too eager. "I'd like that."

"Saturday nights work for everyone?" Bodin suggests, getting to his feet a little unsteadily before stacking our empty dishes and plopping them in the sink with slightly more force than expected. I didn't keep track of how many beers he had, but I'd wager to say he might be a little under the influence.

"Sounds good to me," Ren says, clearing the rest of the table before Bodin can come back and try to do it.

Arran hangs back and lowers his voice. "Is it difficult to get dice like this?"

"You mean the d20? Not really. I can get you some next time I head into Cape Easton for a supply run."

Lowering his voice even further, Arran asks, "Can I borrow it? Until next Saturday?" It's not like Bodin and Ren can't hear him, not with their equally sensitive senses, but many of us have gotten good at pretending we can't in order to give others a modicum of privacy.

For a second, I admire the die's pearlescent hues, so similar to my dragon's scales, and the golden numbers engraved into them. This specific die was a birthday present I gave myself years ago, a one-of-a-kind design. But I don't want to burden Arran with that sentimental knowledge, our strengthening friendship is more important to me.

"Sure," I say, placing the die in his hand. "Though you have to promise to bring it back next week. It's integral to the game."

"I will guard it carefully," Arran says as he turns the die over, his thumb gliding over each side as he studies it.

Bodin shuffles to the door and a somewhat goofy grin pulls at his mouth, making his tusks look more prominent than usual. "Thanks for a great evening. I really had fun with you boys. But now my wife needs me to carry her home and make sweet, sweet love to her until the early morning. Or maybe I need *her* to make love to *me*? But loving shall be had," he declares, looking damn near jolly at the thought. "Maybe tonight is the night I put a baby in her. Wouldn't that be great? Tilly would look so beautiful carrying our child. She'd—" And like a switch has been flipped, Bodin straightens up, his eyes clearing and his skin blanching to a lighter shade of green. He doesn't say anything else, just opens the door and disappears into the night on swift, steady feet.

None of us even deems to wager what that's about, then Arran and Ren are off while I'm left alone with my thoughts, waiting anxiously for Eleanor.

I pace up and down my living room, peering out each window facing the southern hills—from where Eleanor, Audrey, and Viggo will approach to go back to Cape Easton. My heart's in my throat as I debate how I should approach Eleanor, practicing what I should say, and wondering if I should even say anything at all.

Maybe it's better if I let Eleanor go on with her life as is. Without me.

After all, it's been over two decades and she's been fine. I've been fine.

My dragon huffs his frustration at my indecision and pushes against my chest, clearly determined to make his opinion heard. Throughout my life, we've often been at odds, typically only agreeing on Starry Hill and our love for the ocean.

But then I look up and see Eleanor as she comes down the hill, arm hooked through Audrey's and a broad grin on her face as she laughs at something the other woman said. I think back to the game I've designed for my friends and, as Game Master, wonder how I'd encourage the knights to challenge themselves with this chance encounter.

Scales flash down my back and my arms, my feet already moving before my mind has fully processed what I'm going to say. I simply can't waste the opportunity to talk to her at least once more in this lifetime. On this fact, my dragon and I are very much aligned.

CHAPTER 5

I spot Beck before Audrey does, and my stomach does a funny little somersault while my mind blanks. He's actually coming to me. I need to find something smart or witty to say, and quickly, but all my brain wants to supply is noticing how long his strides are and how handsome he looks. *Why do you have to be like this, Eleanor?*

"Becky boy! Fancy seeing you again. Looking fine as always," Audrey drawls, and I can't help the pang of jealousy that stabs at my heart. It's not like I'll stand in their way if they're attracted to each other, but if I had a say, I'd rather have Audrey interested in literally anyone else on this entire planet.

Beck inclines his head toward my tipsy friend, but his eyes stay on me, scanning me from top to bottom. There's nothing lecherous about his gaze, but a small part of me kind of wishes there was.

"Audrey. Welcome back to Starry Hill. Bodin just left here to tend to your cousin." Beck's tone is completely neutral and I quickly look down to hide my tiny smirk at Audrey's inability to rile him.

Swiveling her hips, Audrey elbows me lightly. "Oh yeah. I'm sure he'll be tending her real good all night long."

A small huff of a laugh escapes me because I know she's right. I'm not sure how long the honeymoon phase is supposed to last, but from the way Tilly talked about Bodin tonight, they're very much still in it.

"So, I'm going to give you two a moment to chat while I entertain the moon with a rendition of my favorite song," Audrey says before skipping toward the dock, leaving me alone with Beck before I've had a chance to come up with something charming to say to him.

"Eleanor."

"Beck."

"Hello."

"Hi."

I've never felt more awkward in my life as silence stretches between us, my heart hammering wildly while my mouth refuses to function. How can I be a strong, intelligent woman but when it comes to this beautiful creature in front of me I can't string together a proper sentence? I need Beck to know I actually have a personality underneath this shy layer. It just takes a little bit for me to come out of my shell. Would he have the patience to get to know how I am now?

Wanting to push us out of the awkward zone we've found ourselves in once again, I blurt out, "Have you seen Viggo? I don't have his number and I think I need to get Audrey home before she tries to swim back herself."

"I'll take you." The offer is out of Beck's mouth without a second's hesitation. This late at night, I'd have thought it would be hard to read his expression, but his light eyes shine with sincerity.

"I don't want to put you out like that." I try not to let my relief be too apparent but it's hard when I know a dragon's senses must be much keener than a human's. According to the few articles I've read they can even detect different emotional notes in your scent, as well as having superior eyesight—as was demonstrated when he pointed out Maisie and Ren to me when they were no more than vague dots in the distance.

Beck's already shaking his head. "You're not."

"You sure?" I ask, needing to confirm again. If he suddenly says no, I don't know what I'd do or even how I'd be able to find Viggo. Or would we have to spend the night on the island? I definitely don't want to bother Tilly or Maisie to put us up in their cottages after hearing their very adventurous plans for their partners when they get home.

"Come," Beck says as he pivots and strides toward the wooden dock where Audrey is doing some kind of interpretive dance under the moonlight.

I stare after him for a second, marveling at his glistening white hair and how the moonlight seems to favor him as I futilely smooth my own hair down from the disastrous state it most likely is in right now.

Finally unfreezing my feet from my spot, I hurry my short legs to catch up with Beck. "Thank you for doing this. I really appreciate it."

Beck doesn't owe me anything, but having him willing to take us back to the city in the middle of the night means a lot to me. He might be a little gruffer than he used to be, but it seems he hasn't lost his kind spirit.

Beck looks back at me and slows his pace until we're walking side by side. "It's really okay. It's part of my job."

Oh. *Oh.* I don't want it to hurt, but it does sting. I guess it's good to know *why* he's helping us. If I thought it would be easy to rekindle our dormant friendship or reconnect as quickly as we once did, then at least this dose of reality will help set more realistic expectations.

Reaching for an easy topic instead of letting silence reign again, I ask, "Did you have a good evening with the other guys? Maisie mentioned you hosted a game night?"

A small smile graces Beck's lips and I internally high-five myself. "Yes, thank you. It was my first time having visitors in my home, but I think everyone found it enjoyable. They want to meet weekly to continue the campaign. How was your evening?"

Something squeezes around my heart at the pride in Beck's voice. I'm curious about why it's his first time hosting, but asking any further personal questions might be a bit too presumptuous right now. Instead, I try to keep the conversation light. "Tonight was great. Really special. There are some really wonderful creatures living in Starry Hill."

There's a question in Beck's eyes as he looks at me, but before he has the chance to voice it, Audrey waves a finger between us and asks a little suggestively, "You coming back to Cape Easton with us, stud?"

An almost indiscernible blush stains Beck's cheeks. "I will take you back to the harbor and return home after I've seen to your safety. I imagine Viggo is... preoccupied and might have forgotten."

"Well, who can blame him?" Audrey asks, and I can already feel the mischief brewing in her tone. "Have you seen Juniper? If I had a bunch of tentacles, they'd totally be wrapped around her all the time. And in her. So much penetration would be happening. All the penetration. All the time. I'd be—"

I jump forward and quickly place my finger against her mouth. "Okay," I say loudly, cutting off whatever she was about to describe. "How about we employ that filter of yours for the trip back, pretty please?"

The last thing I need right now is thinking about penetration while I'm attracted to Beck and he's very uninterested in me. I can't even imagine how uncomfortable it must be for him if he scented any of my naughty thoughts while stuck on a small boat in the middle of the dark ocean.

"Ah, fuck. Sorry," Audrey mumbles against my hand, but there's not an ounce of contrition there. "Lips are zipped from here on out. Zippity zipped." She pulls an imaginary line across her lips and locks it with an invisible key as she steps toward

Beck's boat. I have to bite my grin back so she doesn't see how funny I think she is, just in case it eggs her on some more.

Beck steps into his boat and offers his hand to Audrey, who easily jumps down and stretches out along the entirety of the right-side bench with a quick wink toward me. My childhood friend doesn't glance back at her as he keeps his hand out for me, and I curse my nerves as I eye the slightly rocking vessel, contemplating where to place my feet so I don't face-plant onto the sleek deck or fall overboard into the daunting dark water.

Seemingly taking too long, Beck steps closer to me. "I've got you." Before I can ask him what he means, he places his hands around my waist and gently picks me up like I'm a precious doll and not a fully grown, very curvaceous woman who is quite conscious of her weight. I might be short, but I'm not tiny by any standards. But right here, right now, I feel almost delicate in Beck's arms.

"Oh." The word holds my surprise, my thanks, my curiosity, and a feeling I can't quite pinpoint. But when I'm home later, and very much alone, I'm totally replaying this exact moment multiple times.

Reading at least one of my emotions correctly, Beck says, "You're welcome," before carefully letting go of me and directing me to sit on the left while he undoes some knots tying us to the dock so we can sail away from this tranquil island and back to bustling reality.

The ride back is smooth and quiet except for the soft lapping of waves at the vessel as I marvel at the vast expanse of sky above us and the millions of shimmering stars visible without any light pollution out here. Underneath us, the ocean is a velvet navy bed, the surface a dappled mirror of the sky. But despite my usual uneasiness when it comes to the murky depths beneath me, I feel safe. Somehow, I know Beck won't let anything happen to us.

I'm hyperaware of Beck's presence next to me as he guides us back with one hand placed in the water, using some kind of magic to gracefully steer the boat. I want to ask him so many questions, but I also don't want to break this tranquil spell we're in.

Whenever I sneak a look at him, though, I find his gaze already on me.

Much sooner than I'd have liked, the sprawling expanse of Cape Easton comes into view, the city's bright lights a stark contrast to the serenity of Starry Hill. Audrey looks pointedly at me, wordlessly encouraging me to say something to Beck, but I honestly don't know where to start, especially with her assessing eyes on us like that.

Once we glide into the harbor and Beck helps us out, Audrey turns to us with her hands on her hips. "Okay, kids. Either you two talk now or I'm going to lock you in a room together until you've had a proper conversation. I can't stand these awkward silences anymore when you both have so much to catch up on. This is how it's going to work. My blood sugar is getting low, so I'm heading up to the diner and stuffing my face with carbs. Eleanor, I'll wait for you there. But, don't you dare join me until you've both talked, or else."

"Or else what?" I tease, both relieved at her pushing us like this but also not wanting her to get her way too easily.

The glint in Audrey's eye has me second-guessing my comment. "Oh, I've got ideas, don't you worry, but I think you'd prefer having a quiet chat here. Right?"

Beck steps forward and inclines his head toward Audrey. "Thank you for giving us time to talk. I won't keep Eleanor busy for too long."

With a very self-satisfied smirk, Audrey turns on her heels and saunters toward the diner as I stare up at Beck, grateful for him taking the lead, and pleased that it sounds like he wants to actually talk to me too.

"Would you like to sit down?" Beck asks, pointing at a bench seat facing the harbor.

"Sure. It might put us on more equal ground," I try to joke, thinking about the entire foot I'm shorter than Beck.

Walking beside me as we head away from the boat, Beck tilts his head to the side, his shoulder-length hair a moonlit waterfall cascading to one side. "What do you mean?"

"Because you're so tall and I'm so short. There might be less of a difference to look at each other if we're both sitting down," I say, my words getting slower as doubt creeps back in.

Beck shakes his head and states flatly. "I'm not that tall. Bodin is taller than me."

"You're certainly taller than when you were seven," I remark, remembering one of our first summers together when we could still look each other directly in the eye.

"Ah, yes. Puberty changed many things," Beck says with a slight rasp in his voice, his gaze briefly dipping to my breasts as a quick flurry of pearly scales flutters over his cheeks.

"Oh." My breath catches and I quickly divert my eyes from doing a similar sweep down Beck's body. Wanting to change the course of the conversation to a safer topic, I pivot to an apology as he settles onto the bench in front of us. "I'm sorry if Audrey pushed you into talking to me. You really don't have to if you don't want to."

"I want to talk to you," Beck says quickly, the words feeling like a breath of fresh air as he looks up at me with such openness, it makes me let my guard down too.

Sliding onto the bench next to him, I gather my courage and ask, "Why didn't you call me after I gave you my number? It's been months."

A furrow forms between Beck's brows, a look of uncertainty dancing across his face as he stares at me. "I didn't know if you really wanted me to."

"It was implied," I whisper, not feeling angry at him, but perhaps a little hurt. Maybe I didn't expect hugs and an instant full recap of what he's been up to over the years, but I may have entertained the thought that he was almost as excited as me to see each other again.

"I'm not good at reading between the lines," Beck says after a beat. "Creatures can be deceptive with their words sometimes." The statement leaves me nearly breathless because it speaks of ancient hurts that no one deserves. Hurt, I can read in the defeated slump of Beck's shoulders as he studies his shoes. Hurt, I vow to myself I will not inflict on him too.

My friends have taught me a good motto: *If he wanted to, he would.* It's a concept I try to apply to my own lackluster dating life, but I'm now realizing that this concept doesn't necessarily apply to Beck. From what I've heard tonight, he requires direct communication, and expecting him to read my mind won't work if I want to have a chance at rebuilding our friendship.

Tentatively, I reach up and squeeze his shoulder. "I'm sorry. It's a cruel world sometimes."

Beck presses his lips together and accepts the apology with a nod. "It is, but it's not your fault."

"It's not yours either."

For the first time, we lapse into a comfortable silence as we look out over the harbor and the boats peacefully bobbing in place.

Beck clears his throat. "So, you want me to call you this week?"

I turn sideways in my seat so he can read my sincerity. "Yes. But only if you want to."

Beck mirrors my position and his ocean eyes shine with an emotion I can't quite place. "I do. I want us to be friends again. You were my best friend before."

"You were mine too." Taking a fortifying breath, I look at Beck's kind face and ask the question that's been weighing on me for years. "Where did you go, Beck? One day we were playing in the backyard, pushing each other on the swing, making up dances, and having fun, and the next day, you were just gone. I went to ask your grandmother where you were, but she said you had to leave early. She wouldn't give me a reason why you didn't say goodbye. Every summer I waited for you, hoping to see you one more time."

Pain flashes across Beck's face and he lifts his hand toward mine before laying it back in his lap and curling it into a fist, scales glimmering on his knuckles. "I did go back for you. Eventually. I went to see you the day after I graduated."

I press my hand to my chest, my heart aching all over again as if no time has passed since that morning he disappeared, that missed opportunity at seeing him slicing through me like a sharp knife. "You did? I never knew. I graduated a year early and moved to Youngford to study law, then moved to Cape Easton a couple of years ago."

Beck swallows audibly. "Would you...?"

"Would I what?" I encourage, trying to stay present in this moment so I can properly crash out at home once I process everything he's said tonight.

Looking adorably awkward, Beck tucks a strand of moonlit blond hair behind his ear. "Would you want to hang out sometime? Get coffee together? Or lemonade, if it's still your favorite?"

I smile and twirl a piece of hair around my index finger, feeling like he's almost asking me out on a date. Beck might not have meant the offer to sound romantic, so in order to avoid any misunderstandings, I refuse to read too much into it and simply take his words at face value. "I'd really like that. We can meet here in the city, or maybe you can show me around Starry Hill?"

Beck's entire body stills, his eyes rounding as he searches my face. "You want to come back to Starry Hill?" he asks, hope blossoming in his voice.

I nod as a lightness settles in my heart. "Very much. Lucille invited me to visit her next weekend at The Dancing Daisy. We could hang out after, if you're free?"

"I'm free," Beck answers quickly, a flurry of glittering scales rushing across his arms. "I'll come pick you up in the morning and drop you off again when you're ready to go back."

"You sure it won't be a bother to go twice? Maybe I can ask Viggo to do one of the trips?" I suggest.

"Please don't." It's a simple request from Beck, one that's very easy for me to agree to.

"Okay," I breathe, hardly containing my smile.

"Okay," Beck repeats, his eyes grazing across my face like he's memorizing each one of my features.

"Saturday?" I state more than ask, already wondering how I'm going to get through the week when I have such an exciting weekend filled with a trip to Starry Hill, a visit to a bookshop, and Beck waiting for me at the end of it.

"Saturday," Beck replies with a brilliant smile that matches my own.

BECK

CHAPTER 6

Deliberately making my footsteps more pronounced so they can signal my arrival and not startle Lucille, I clear my throat as an added measure before knocking on the open door of The Dancing Daisy.

"Beck, right on time, as always." The octogenarian greets me with a kind smile and ushers me inside her shop. Shelves of books line the walls, and even if they're not in alphabetical order, I do believe Lucille has some kind of organization system for them.

I eye the colorful display of magical treats and candies at the back of the shop, and note which cases are emptier than others.

"Did you order more stock for those I need to pick up in the city, or do you still have enough in storage that I can use to refill them for you?"

"No need to worry about that now. Tea first," Lucille says as she shoos me toward my favorite orange leather chair in the reading corner. She pours us each a cup of strong tea while I place a loaf of freshly baked rye bread on the table between us. As is our weekly tradition, I take the rattling cup out of her hands and wait for her to take a seat in her matching chair before I sit down next to her.

There was never a spoken conversation or a written rule for our weekly meetings. What started as scheduled monthly appointments to talk about her orders for her shop evolved into more frequent visits after the loss of her husband, Lochan—a jovial cyclops who was just as beloved by the Starry Hill community as Lucille.

Eventually, I started coming by early every Saturday morning before the other shops would open and we follow the same routine each time. Lucille brews us some tea and I bring her bread, and we sit in the high-backed chairs and talk about everything and nothing before going about our normal days. And now, I wouldn't miss our Saturday dates for anything.

"What's on the schedule for today?" Lucille asks as she lifts her cup toward her mouth, lightly blowing on the hot tea before taking a tentative sip from the dainty, floral cup. There's a hint of a smile in the shape of her lips and something new in her gaze I can't quite place.

Ignoring the unusual expression, I go through my list. "I'm heading to Cape Easton to pick up an order of ingredients for Richard and Annamae from a bake store, then visiting the pharmacy for an order for Samara." I take a quick sip of tea and stare toward the window out front as I mumble quickly against my cup, "And then picking up Eleanor so she can spend the morning with you here."

At the sound of Eleanor's name, my dragon jolts upright in my chest, flickers of scales spreading across my body with his excitement to see her again—excitement I very much share even if I'm trying to play it cool.

Keeping my eyes straight ahead, I casually lift my hand to cover the side of my neck where the appearance of scales might be most obvious. I hope the move was subtle enough to not draw Lucille's attention toward it, wanting to avoid the slew of questions that would surely follow. Today feels very important and I'm not quite ready to share with anyone what it means to me to reconnect with Eleanor.

Even though more than twenty years have passed, I've never forgotten her or the joy she brought to my life. Every so often, I'd spot someone with a similar shade of hair, only to be disappointed when I didn't recognize any features when they turned around.

Having the opportunity now to get to know Eleanor again, to see if there's a trace of that easy friendship we used to have—maybe more if I'm truly honest with myself—it feels like a second chance at something special that I'd never even dare to dream up for myself.

Could my luck finally have changed? Is fate finally smiling down on me? It's too early to say, but I'm holding on to that thread of hope with both hands.

Throughout my life, I've had other friends, but no one has been able to replace that easy connection Eleanor and I once had, one without any weight of expectations, or duties, or responsibilities.

After I took Eleanor back to Cape Easton last weekend, it took me two days to gather the courage to call her. At first, there were a few stumbling attempts of accidentally talking over each other, but we slowly fell into a comfortable rhythm, one very similar to when we were young. We reminisced about old times, laughed at jokes we told as kids, but never crossed the line toward any serious topics, nor did we venture to talk about how we lost contact. It's like we're rebuilding our connection, brick by brick, and I'm nervous about saying something that might make the wall crumble and possibly lose her forever. I don't want to do anything that'll jeopardize that.

For so long, I've craved someone who can see me as me, not as a dragon, or a ferryman, not as a guardian, or any other label I've been given in my life—just me. Beck Shinsu.

Talking to Eleanor reminded me of who I was before I was weighed down by the expectations of others, or carried the responsibility of the safekeeping of an entire community, and by the end of our long phone call I felt lighter, happier, and perhaps a little less lonely too. Hopeful.

Lucille taps a finger against her cup, the smile in her voice evident as she says, "I am so looking forward to seeing that dear girl again. She was lovely when I met her. And a booklover to boot."

"She is. And she's very excited to see The Dancing Daisy and talk about books with you," I say, not realizing the words are out of my mouth by the time the whole sentence is complete.

Lowering her cup, Lucille's grin grows. "And, pray tell, how did you come by this information, dear dragon boy?"

I swallow the last dregs of my tea in one gulp and quickly, but carefully, place my cup back on the table. "Well, would you look at the time? I best be going. I'll bring Eleanor by a little later and help you with that stock," I promise, already backing away toward the entrance.

Lucille lifts her hand in greeting as her gaze softens. "I won't press you for anything you don't want to tell me, Beck. But I'm always here if you want to talk. About anything."

Bowing my head, I utter a soft, "Thank you." It might be rude of me to flee from the conversation, but I'm not ready to share yet. Not until Eleanor and I have a steady foundation again. I know Lucille will understand that when I do eventually tell her.

I slip down the small passage between The Dancing Daisy and The Lonely Rake, and take the back way down Starry Hill, away from the shops and any other conversations I'm not ready for. I need to get to Cape Easton as fast as possible so I can start picking up those orders. The earlier I can get done with my errands, the earlier I can focus on Eleanor.

Time passes quickly and slowly at the same time as I navigate the city streets and gather the things our town needs, depositing them in my boat before I settle onto a bench that overlooks the harbor, the same bench Eleanor and I sat on last weekend.

I stare down at the old phone in my hand, wondering if I should call Eleanor to see if she's going to be on time, or sit here and wait for her to show up. On the island, we hardly use phones, the signal being spotty and no one really needing one. But for me, it is a necessity with my job, something I didn't ever think I'd be grateful for until this past week.

Before I can spiral too far, my dragon bolts upright, practically panting as he calls my attention to a familiar scent in the air.

My head snaps up.

She's here.

Standing in a flowy blue dress with delicate straps tied over her shoulders, Eleanor looks gorgeous. The fabric hugs her in all the right places, spanning tight across full breasts that have me salivating. Her hair looks soft and shiny, hanging down her back in a radiant copper curtain, my fingers begging to comb through the long, silky strands.

Be cool, please, I tell my dragon while also admonishing the direction of my own thoughts. *Remember, we're friends. Just friends. Go easy with all the scales. We don't want to scare her off.*

I force myself not to rush forward, and simply stand up and approach her at an intentionally measured pace I've seen Bodin use with Tilly. I might be three years older than Bodin, but socially, I know I'm far behind my friends and can use any behaviors I've observed their partners find favorable. Not that Eleanor is my partner. She's my friend. But it's been a very long time since I've cared this much about what someone thought of me. I want—no, *need*—to do everything right with her.

With every step closer, the fragrant blend of blooming lavender and sparkling water wraps around my senses, igniting nostalgia for when I first scented her when we were seven, but now holding a distinctly more feminine quality that calms me as much as it makes my heart race.

"Hi," I say a little breathlessly, inclining my head in a greeting as I come to a stop about a yard from Eleanor.

"Hello," Eleanor says with a small smile, tucking some of her fiery hair behind her ear. "Thank you for picking me up today."

"It's no problem. I had some errands to run in the city this morning."

"Oh, I see," Eleanor says, her smile slipping as she stares at her shoes. I don't know what I said wrong, but I don't like doing anything that'll make her lose her smiles. I want to give her reasons to smile. I want to *be* the reason for her smiles.

"You look pretty," I blurt out, gesturing at her dress. It's quite the understatement but I don't want to bombard her with all my thoughts.

Pink blooms across Eleanor's cheeks and her scent blossoms, my dragon rolling onto his back as he breathes it in. "Thank you. I don't normally wear dresses, but something about Starry Hill makes me want to try new things."

"That's good?" I ask, unsure of what it means.

Eleanor holds my eyes as she nods. "I think it is. Here, I brought you something."

While she reaches inside her tote bag, a thousand thoughts flit through my brain, scrambling the neatly organized way I make sense of the world.

"You got me something?" I ask, surprised and curious and very much delighted. It's not even my birthday and Eleanor surely knows that. I still remember her birthday. Not that I expect her, or anyone, to get me anything then, but the thought of someone giving me something just because they wanted to is kind of throwing me off-balance. In a good way, I think.

"Of course," Eleanor says easily, producing two brown paper bags. "I know we talked about our shared love for bread the other night and I mentioned that café close to my office? Well, I went there this morning and I couldn't pick which of my favorites I wanted you to try first, so I got you both. I thought if you liked them, you could maybe share them with the boys later at game night?" Eleanor adds shyly, her voice becoming quieter as she hands me the bread.

My dragon pushes against my chest, nudging me forward to comfort Eleanor, to put her at ease and make her feel safe with us. It's something I've not experienced since...

Shoving him down, I stare at Eleanor for perhaps a little too long before I whisper, "I didn't have time to make anything for tonight yet."

Eleanor smiles at me like she expected me to say that, but there's no judgment there, just understanding. "I thought you might be busy with picking me up and all that."

Swallowing against the odd lump in my throat, I rasp out, "That's really thoughtful of you. Thank you. Is this the cranberry orange sourdough you mentioned?"

"Yes. And this is the walnut cinnamon sourdough."

I open the bags and lower my nose to take in the delicious aroma wafting from the bread as we fall into step next to each and head down the dock together, chatting about marmalade pairings for each bread and flavor combinations I'd like to try one day. When we get to the boat, I hop in first and secure the bread in the hull before returning to help Eleanor down.

Her honey-brown eyes assess the boat and her heartbeat speeds up, but I refrain from commenting on it. I don't want to do or say anything that might be construed as negative.

Instead, I reach out and place my hands around Eleanor's waist before I gently set her down in the boat. Eleanor grabs onto my arms as the boat balances out, and my brain sort of freezes. My whole body freezes. My dragon freezes too. She's so beautiful and having her right here in my arms feels like a dream come true. I don't think I'm able to let go.

"Thank you," Eleanor says brightly as she steps out of my arms and goes to sit on the starboard side while I try to find my bearings.

As I go through the motions of getting everything ready to set sail, untying the boat from the cleats, my dragon and I scanning our surroundings for any threats or obstacles, I find my calm in the routine and my normal senses eventually return.

I relax into my seat on the port side and lean down to place a hand in the water. The moment I touch the ocean, all my anxieties melt away and my dragon stretches out within my chest.

We're not going swimming now, sorry. Don't want to scare Eleanor. Maybe tomorrow morning before anyone else is awake, I tell him through our mental bond as I navigate our way through the harbor.

Once we pass all the boats and glide into the open waters of Indigo Bay, I send more power into my hand and direct us toward the current that'll take us straight to Starry Hill.

The beauty of my magic is that the more I give the ocean, the more she gives back to me. It's a wonderful relationship we've been building since I discovered my gift all those years ago. As much as I guard Starry Hill, I also guard the ocean surrounding our little island, and she takes care of me too.

My skin tingles and my heart races as the ocean pushes us forward, my hair whipping out behind me as I embrace the freedom of the open ocean. A lazy smile stretches across my dragon's sharp jaw as he lifts his head and breathes in the salty air mixed with hints of Eleanor's lavender and water scent, a smile that's echoed on my own face too.

I don't know when I closed my eyes to savor this feeling, but when I open them, I find Eleanor watching me with a soft, unblinking gaze, her jaw slack and one hand on her chest as she releases a slow breath.

CHAPTER 7

"Knock, knock," I call as I rap my knuckles against the bright yellow door, the color reminding me of the fresh pollen in the center of a happy daisy.

"Eleanor, dear, is that you?" Lucille calls, popping her head out from behind a display rack of scrapbooking supplies.

My jaw drops as I step inside The Dancing Daisy and take in the artfully quaint interior. I gape at the bookish knickknacks squeezed onto shelves filled to the brim with familiar and yet-to-be-loved titles, at the tasteful sage-green accents scattered throughout the old stone building, and the joyous way the morning sun trickles in through the paned front window, the light dancing across the earthy rug at the room's center.

I've never believed in love at first sight. Until now.

Everything about The Dancing Daisy is perfect.

It feels like I'm standing in the middle of someone's cozy living room, but better, because at the back of the building I spy colorful jars filled with candy I've never seen in my life before, and I'm already salivating at the thought of tasting them.

"Oh, I know that look," Lucille says as she shuffles toward me. "I had a similar one the first time I saw this old shop, even if it didn't quite look like this back then."

"It's..." No fitting words enter my mind, so I resort to gesturing, flailing my arms in a way that I hope expresses just how charming I think The Dancing Daisy is. A glimmer of thankfulness races through me that none of my coworkers are here to witness me acting in such an uncomposed, unlawyery manner.

"I know, dear. I know," Lucille sighs gently, coming to stand next to me as I rake my gaze across every tiny detail I can see so I can imprint this vision into my mind forever.

Peering behind me, Lucille asks, "Is Beck not with you?"

The question snaps me back to the present and I turn to face her. "No, sorry. He had to drop some things off at The Sparkling Cauldron for Samara."

"That boy works too hard," Lucille tuts affectionately. The genuine concern in her voice burrows into my heart and solidifies Lucille's place as one of my new favorite people in Starry Hill.

"I've definitely gotten that impression too." Leaning toward her, I whisper conspiratorially, "He almost tried to carry all the ingredients he got in Cape Easton to The Flowering Teapot this morning, but luckily Bodin showed up in time with his cart to help."

Brows drawn down, Lucille takes one of my hands in hers. "Beck has such a good heart. A pure spirit. And it doesn't take a magical creature to see it. I'm confident your beautiful human eyes can see it as clearly as my old ones do."

I nod. "They sure can, but it's good to have it confirmed."

Wait, is Lucille trying to wingwoman me?

Despite how much I like Beck, we've only reconnected like a week ago. I don't really know him. Not adult Beck, anyway. But having Lucille vouch for him makes me even happier to have him back in my life. Neither of us is the same person we were as children, but I'm glad to hear that Beck's still the same at his core as he was back then.

Hooking her arm through mine, Lucille beams at me and leads me deeper into the shop. "I think that's enough talk about boys—for now. Let me give you a tour of my cozy slice of heaven."

Lucille shows me everything, from the way she categorizes the books to how she curates which to put on display. We talk stationery and compare annotation techniques, then she gives me a quick rundown of the magical candy against the back wall. I'm not brave enough for any of them today, but maybe another time I'd try the one that changes your lip color.

Once we've listed some of our favorite books and established we're both fans of a good mystery or anything fantasy related as long as there's a substantial romance arc included, we make our way over to the high-backed chairs in a nook toward the back. A darling teapot with two matching cups and saucers wait on a table for us with some slices of rye bread.

Pouring Lucille's cup for her, I say, "This is the most enchanting bookshop I've ever seen. Honestly. It's such a warm, inviting literary haven. How long have you had it?"

Cradling her cup, Lucille's gaze turns wistful. "I can't take all the credit for The Dancing Daisy. It was in my Lochan's family long before we fell in love and I joined him here on the island. We spruced it up over the years and tried to stay relevant, making sure we stock a mix of classics and new releases. My Lochan gave it fresh coats of paint whenever I had another whim of an idea, and we added tiny treasures we found to give it a more homely atmosphere so that anyone entering through that yellow door would feel welcome."

Every word from Lucille holds me captive, the love for her husband woven into every happy crinkle around her eyes when she mentions his name. It's clear that The Dancing Daisy is not just a shop, it's a labor of love passed down from a previous generation and cultivated into a hearth for book lovers.

Lucille dabs gently at her eyes before continuing, "But if I can be a little frank with you, lately it has been getting more challenging for me to manage it all. After Lochan passed, and considering my age, it's not always easy to do everything by myself anymore. I love The Dancing Daisy and everything it represents more than I can express, but we're not as effective as we once were. Plus, I'm the only human-run shop on the hill and by far the weakest in strength. Luckily I'm part of this wonderful community, and a few of the strapping young lads are always willing to come help me out with some heavy lifting when needed."

If I didn't like Lucille before, I undoubtedly do now. Not only is she resilient but her positive outlook on life has me wanting to reassess how I view the world. I've been so caught up in a cold corporate life, forcing my very round self into a prescribed square hole, that I've forgotten that not everyone is as buttoned-up and aloof as the people I work with on a daily basis. If there is a way I can escape from that, even for just a little bit at a time, and surround myself with more people like Lucille—and Beck—I want to do that.

Reaching over to take her hand, I say, "First of all, I am so sorry for your loss. It sounds like your Lochan was lovely and the perfect partner for you. I can't imagine how difficult it must be for you after experiencing and losing such great love. And second of all, we're friends now, right? As far as I know, friends help friends, and I therefore volunteer my Saturdays to The Dancing Daisy. I'd love to come help you out if you don't mind having me around?"

Lucille fixes her watery gaze on me. "Thank you, Eleanor dear. That's awfully sweet of you, but I wouldn't be able to pay you."

I'm already shaking my head. "You don't need to. It would be my honor and an absolute pleasure to come out here on Saturday mornings. I can research trending books for you during the week and then we can brainstorm ideas on how to breathe some fresh life into the shop, maybe plan some bookish events for the community? I want to support you in any way I can. But if I'm overstepping, please tell me. I don't want to do anything you're not comfortable with."

"Eleanor, I'm sure my Lochan sent you to me at the perfect time. Now, let me go get something a little stronger we can add to the tea and then we can toast this new partnership of ours."

Shifting onto the edge of my seat, I watch Lucille's retreating form, my heart drumming giddily, excited about my life for the first time in longer than I care to think about.

Lucille and I work all morning—planning, organizing, and chatting. I hang onto every word she says as she tells me the detailed history of The Dancing Daisy, how it got its name, and how she and Lochan met while she shows me where everything in the shop is kept and how it works. After lunch, she shoos me away so I can head to Beck's mill and spend the afternoon with him before I have to go back to the city.

My entire body buzzes as I walk across the island's rolling green hills, my mind still trying to process the morning's events. This feels like a pivotal moment in my life and I don't want to blink too hard in case this isn't real.

Coming out to Starry Hill on Saturdays, spending the day surrounded by books in the coziest shop I've ever seen, and learning from someone as wise and warm as Lucille, is more than I could've ever wished for myself.

ELEANOR

CHAPTER 8

When I crest the most northern hill leading toward the dock and Beck's home, I spot him opening his front door like he knew I was coming. The way his entire face lights up the moment our eyes meet does some funny things to my heart, and my answering grin matches his.

"Hi. I hope I'm not interrupting your schedule," I say when I'm within human hearing distance, hastily checking my watch.

Beck shakes his head, his smile still in place as I come to a stop in front of him. "You're not, but even if you were interrupting something else, I'd still be happy to see you."

My heart practically skips a beat as he meets my eyes. "Me too," I admit. "I was just asking because I remember how aware you were of time when we were small and you always liked sticking to a schedule. Maybe you still do?"

Tilting his head to the side, Beck stares at me with unguarded curiosity. "You remember more about me than I thought you would."

I shrug and study my sandals in an attempt to hide the color rising to my cheeks. "I could say the same about you. Like the other night when you asked me if I still write notes in the margins of books. And how much I like lemonade."

A few charged seconds stretch between us before Beck brings the conversation back to neutral ground. "How was Lucille? Do you like the shop?"

My head snaps up and I jokingly touch the back of my hand to my forehead. "Do you have a couch? I think I might swoon if I start thinking about how perfect The Dancing Daisy is."

Beck instantly steps backward and holds the door open for me. "Oh yes. Come in. The couch is in the living room, straight through here."

I mentally smack myself on the forehead for confusing Beck with my stupid choice of words and renew my silent vow to be more careful with my phrasing as I stop to take in the interior of his home.

It's otherworldly. Ancient. Masculine. And yet, homely.

Exposed brown stone walls surround us on all sides, and a large pillar juts up from the open-plan ground floor, through the mezzanine level and up to the soaring ceiling with wooden beams running across it. Against the right side of the pillar is a giant gear that controls the water mill on the outside.

My eyes drift toward the kitchen, the medieval fireplace and antique stove where I imagine Beck creates his breads. Pots and pans hang from hooks against one wall and large windows let in warm light, the ocean an ever-present companion to this old cottage.

Turning toward him, I say, "You have a really nice home. It looks like it has a rich history."

"I'm happy you like it," Beck says, relief bleeding into his tone as he lowers himself down onto the edge of the large kitchen table. "It's one of the oldest homes on the island."

"You know what?" I ask, stepping toward the living room, spying his game setup, hand-drawn map, and empty glasses waiting on the table for tonight, savoring all these little glimpses of who Beck is and what he values.

Beck hangs back in the kitchen, arms folded across his chest. "What?"

"I think... I never imagined a grown-up version of you. You somehow remained stuck at twelve in my mind, like the last time I saw you. You're definitely not twelve anymore." This mature version of Beck may not be what I expected, but it's so much better. Turning to meet his gaze, I brush some hair behind my ear before I add softly, "Thank you for inviting me here. I'm glad to get to know you again at this time in our lives."

"It's really nice to have you here. My oldest friend in my old home," Beck says, his eyes not leaving me for a second as his pearlescent scales luster in the afternoon light streaming in through the kitchen window.

I've never believed in fate or unknown powers controlling my life, but it feels like the universe is somehow conspiring in our favor to bring us back together again at this specific point in our lives. I don't know what it means, yet, but for the first time in more years than I care to count, there's a tiny effervescent bubble sitting in my chest, really excited about the future.

Leaning against the thick pillar, I say sheepishly, "I'm really sorry about earlier, the fainting thing was a manner of speaking and not a real situation. It's just that I adore The Dancing Daisy and my brain is still spinning with everything I've seen and heard today."

"That's okay," Beck says, bracing his arms comfortably behind him, inadvertently putting his broad shoulders on display. "When you didn't immediately run to the couch, I figured I might have misunderstood."

"Still, I'll take more care with my words in the future," I promise both Beck and myself.

"Me too."

Fidgeting with the fabric of my dress, I look down and try not to ogle those shoulders. But I have eyes and this girl is weak.

You're friends, I remind myself. *New friends. Technically old friends who are new friends again. But friends. And friends don't ogle friends.*

Clearing my throat so I can interrupt my own thoughts, I start hesitantly, "Talking about the future, I might have a favor to ask you."

"Anything," Beck states, the word sounding like a promise.

I take a deep breath, squash down my insecurities as much as they'd let me, and explain, "Well, Lucille and I have cooked up some plans for the shop and I'll need to come out here more often. Like, every Saturday. Do you think it's possible for you to pick me up again next weekend? And maybe the weekend after? For a while?"

"Of course. Anytime. For as long as you need me." The words come effortlessly, and the relaxed set to those shoulders makes me believe he really means it. Still, I never want to take advantage of his generosity.

Before I can start doubting myself about inconveniencing him again, Beck asks, "What kind of plans do you have for the bookshop?"

I pad over to the kitchen and pull out a chair on the opposite side of the table as I explain, "We're still busy brainstorming a couple of ideas and we'll need to see if they're practical in the Starry Hill setting, but our first plan we decided on is starting a book club. We'll do a trial run with one pick and if there's some interest we can expand it to other genres. My task this week is to find a good mystery book that other residents might like. If Lucille approves, I'll try to design some flyers so we can start telling other residents about it."

Beck hops down from the table and pulls out the seat next to mine, his brow furrowed as he looks at me. "Aren't you very busy at your lawyer job? When will you have time for it all?"

Appreciating his concern, I pat the top of his hand. "Trust me, I'll be using every single thing related to The Dancing Daisy as a coping mechanism to get through my week. I'm already looking forward to next Saturday. But that's enough about me. How are you? What do you have planned for the boys and their knights later?"

I track a flurry of sparkles cresting down Beck's forearm as he rests it on the table, his eyes following the scales before they disappear under his skin again. He frowns down at his smooth arm before shifting his gaze back to me.

"We have our first battle coming up. I'm going to be nice tonight and challenge them with a small fight so they can practice using their ability scores to try to control the narrative. I'll leave the twists and larger battles for another week when they're more settled into the game."

"That sounds like a really good plan from what sounds like a thoughtful Game Master," I say, hoping Beck hears the sincerity in my compliment. Judging by what he's told me on the phone and the map and files laid out on the gaming table, Beck is not only diligent but a skilled narrator too.

Leaning forward, Beck asks, "Do you want to play?"

I'm quick to shake my head. "Oh no, I don't want to intrude. You boys have fun while I go curl up with a book at home and get started on my research for book club."

"But you know Knights and Castles isn't a game for only guys, right?" Beck's eyes implore me to understand, his slumped shoulders pulling on every single one of my heartstrings.

I don't know who messed with him and made him lose confidence in voicing his opinions, I just know I never want to meet them. We'd totally have words. They might even deserve a slap. Or two.

Tamping down my anger, I focus on reassuring Beck, laying a gentle hand on his forearm. "Totally. Maybe I can join in on a future campaign if the others don't mind me playing?"

"I'd like that," Beck says, staring down at my hand for a second before placing his on top of mine.

Our gazes meet as I reply softly, "Me too."

Two months of a similar routine passes by in no time at all. Beck picks me up on Saturday mornings once he's finished gathering the island's orders, and I bring him bread to try from different bakeries I like. Then, we have a quiet boat ride while I marvel at him without trying to make it too obvious. The way Beck relaxes while he steers such a large vessel by simply placing his hand in the water truly intrigues me.

With each additional trip, my fear of the ocean melts away a little quicker until my nerves are simmering at a manageable level—a level I hope doesn't bother Beck anymore. He's never said anything but I've noticed he does this adorable nose twitch when my heart beats extra fast, so it's clear that he's aware of my nerves even if he's been nice enough not to mention them.

We talk often, at least twice a week on the phone now, and I find myself craving more time in Starry Hill and more time with him. I've never been a huge fan of Cape Easton, and certainly not my job, but leaving the island each Saturday afternoon, right when the sunset is at its prettiest and my heart feels the fullest, is becoming more difficult with each week that passes.

As the sun touches the horizon and Beck walks me to my car in the harbor's parking lot, I nearly drag my feet, not quite ready to say goodbye. I know Beck's friends will be waiting for him if I keep him too long, so I tamp down the inconvenient flutters in my stomach as I wrestle with the words I've been practicing all week.

"Thank you for bringing me back. Again. You still sure you don't mind the trip twice every Saturday?"

"I told you not to ask me that again. You know I'm always happy to see you," Beck states matter-of-factly, unknowingly igniting those butterflies once again.

A warm breeze gusts between us and I quickly clutch at my dress with both hands, not wanting to show the whole harbor what underwear I have on. When I look up at Beck through the hair whipped across my face, he's already got one tentative hand reached out.

I forget to breathe as Beck gently brushes his fingertips against my face and pushes the strands behind my ear. My heart speeds up as he holds my gaze, momentarily dipping his eyes to my mouth before his nose twitches, then swiftly placing both hands in his pockets.

I swallow while I try to collect myself and finally push the practiced words out in the most nonchalant way I can manage. "Next Saturday, if you have errands to run in the city again before we're meant to meet up, maybe I can go with you?"

Beck quirks his head to the side. "You'd want to do that? With me? Even if it's boring?"

"Well, yes. I could help you source some of the items too, if you want? Use my vast city-girl knowledge for the good of Starry Hill. And it could be nice to squeeze in a little more time together. Again, only if you want. But I also understand if you don't." *Stop talking, Eleanor. Rambling is not cute,* I scold myself. *Articulate clearly and concisely, that's the way to get yourself heard,* my mother's voice echoes in my head.

Just before my shoulders curl with embarrassment, Beck bends down to meet me at eye level. "You mean that? You really like spending time with me that much?" he asks, his pale blue eyes holding so much hope it makes my heart ache. In this moment, Beck looks completely vulnerable, and I know it's an honor that he lets his guard down so easily around me.

I resist the desire to brush a lock of pale blond hair behind his ear, and clutch my tote tighter to me instead. "Why wouldn't I?"

Beck's silent for a while as he stares down at me, his gaze flitting all over my face. "No one... I've never... I mean... Yes. That would be nice. Really nice. Thank you."

I press my lips together, trying to contain my smile as I mumble, "You're welcome. Now get going before the other boys eat all of that yummy brioche. I'll see you next week."

"Yes. Saturday. Call you Monday?" Beck asks, needing to confirm with me the same way he always does before saying goodbye.

I take a quick fortifying breath and, hoping it doesn't sound too forward, say, "Whenever you want."

Beck rubs at the scales on his neck. "I don't think I can call you on my way back."

"What?"

He shrugs. "I like talking to you. So if I was allowed to call you whenever I want, we'd be on the phone all day. Including while I'm on the boat on the way back to Starry Hill. The guys said I should give you a little space, but also not too much. That's why I thought Monday might be okay."

Don't read too much into it, Eleanor. He's just being thoughtful. "You could call me on Sundays, too?" I suggest cautiously. "I go grocery shopping in the morning and do some chores around the house in the afternoon. Nothing too exciting. In the evenings I just read. You can call then?"

The biggest, most radiant grin I've seen to date spreads across Beck's face. "Okay. I'll talk to you tomorrow."

"Tomorrow," I confirm, my heart feeling lighter than a feather being swept on the wings of the wind.

Life is looking good lately. Really good.

Beck

CHAPTER 9

Heart still racing and unable to sleep after being on the phone with Eleanor again tonight, I shrug on a shirt and head out my door. My dragon wakes up from his slumber and turns his head eagerly toward the moon, gently pushing me toward the gleaming silver light dancing on the ripples of the dark ocean.

Sorry, not now. I need to think. Maybe tomorrow we can go for a swim again, I promise him vaguely, not really in the mood to get in the water this late. My dragon huffs in protest, but doesn't argue, just turns his back on me and curls up in a far corner of my chest.

Stars blink at me from above as I follow the coastline down toward the east. Darkened cottages peek out between the hills, their inhabitants most likely blissfully asleep by now. The entire island is quiet except for the muffled thuds of my long strides as my mind wrestles with my heart.

Since Eleanor reentered my life, I've been happier than I've ever been before—including when we were kids. I constantly hunger for more time with her, more *everything* with her, but I don't know how to go about it or if I'm being too greedy. All I know is that she consumes my thoughts all day and all night, my dreams now too.

Even when she's not around, I can hear her laughter. The sweet cadence of her voice is ingrained in my memory like a favorite song. When I close my eyes, her face appears on my darkened lids, her striking red hair luring me closer, my fingers itching to card through her long locks, tilt her face up to mine and finally press my lips to hers like I've been longing to do.

But I'm nervous, more nervous than I've been about anything else. What if I scare Eleanor off if I reveal the direction that my feelings have gone? It's wonderful being her friend, but I want more. So much more with her. But I simply can't lose her again. I don't think I'd survive that.

The distant rumbling of male voices has me searching the horizon for their source, and my dragon opens a sleepy eye to help me determine if they're friend or foe. Nostrils flaring, we quickly sniff the air to pinpoint their location and identities, relaxing again once we recognize Arran and Bodin's familiar scents. My dragon stretches his long, serpentine body, yawning languidly before curling up into a tight ball again and drifting off to sleep, while I continue forward to join my friends.

I lengthen my strides as Bodin lifts a hand in greeting, beckoning me closer to where he's sitting with Arran on the front steps of the vampire's castle.

"Beck. You're out late," Bodin says, patting a spot next to him.

I shrug and keep standing, unable to sit while my mind is still preoccupied. "I could say the same about you."

"It seems as if my home has become some type of refuge for wayward creatures tonight," Arran says, hardly looking up as he continues tinkering with something small in his hands.

A sly smile pulls at Bodin's mouth, which I recognize as a sign of teasing to come, but thankfully not in my direction this time.

"You know, that isn't a bad idea," Bodin drawls. "Your castle is big, and I imagine a little lonely too. You could consider opening your doors to host some creatures."

"Foolish talk," Arran mumbles, shooting a severe frown Bodin's way.

As Starry Hill's founder and longest resident, Arran mostly keeps to himself, only coming out after sunset to gather his much-needed blood bags from The Bandaged Heart before returning to the castle he built with his own hands. I don't know how long it's been since he's fed directly from a source, but I do frequent trips to the blood bank in the city to ensure he has an adequate supply that'll keep him nourished.

When he joined our boys' night on the beach many months ago, and taught us log-throwing techniques, we were all pleased to get to know a new side of him. I initially didn't expect him to accept my invitation to join our Knights and Castles game, but I'm really enjoying his company and have come to think of him as a friend.

Gesturing at the object in Arran's hands, I ask, "What are you making?"

"Dice."

Arran hands me the d20 die and I hold it up to the moonlight to see the details more clearly. It's completely hand-carved, the edges sanded smooth with numbers engraved into each side. It's from the same sandstone his castle is made of and must've taken ages to create.

Turning the die over in my hand, I gawp at his fine handiwork. "This is amazing. How long did it take you to carve this?"

"This one, not that long. I borrowed your die that first game night so I could sketch out the design before trying my hand at making my own. This is the fourth one I've made."

"Fourth?" Bodin asks, sounding just as astonished as me as he takes the die and studies it just as closely as I had.

Arran rubs a hand over his cropped hair. "Aye, a little memento for each of us. Thought it might be nice to have something to commemorate our game nights. Besides, there's not much to do when you're awake while the rest of the island sleeps. Except for you two tonight, that is."

"But you have sunscreen now. You can go out anytime of the day and do other stuff," I point out logically.

Arran gives me a smile that doesn't quite reach his eyes. "Old habits and all that."

"Change could be good for you," Bodin suggests, leaning back against the wall, arms crossed over his chest as he gives both me and Arran very loaded looks.

I don't know why he wants to include me in that statement, so I ignore the implication, choosing to direct the conversation toward something more important. "If you're up for change, maybe you'll finally let us install power for your castle?" Out of all the homes and shops on Starry Hill, Arran's is the only one that doesn't have electricity, despite Bodin and me offering to bring him into the present century numerous times.

Arran waves a dismissive hand and scoffs, "I have gone without modern luxuries or any kinds of technology for over four hundred years. I don't foresee myself developing a sudden need now, or at any point within the next four hundred."

Not seeing how I can argue with that line of thinking, I point my chin toward Bodin. "Why are you here? I thought you hardly ever leave Tilly's side."

"I'd also like to know," Arran says. "You hadn't said a word until Beck arrived, simply sagged onto the step beside me in grumpy silence."

Bodin runs his fingers through his beard and mumbles, "Uhm... Tilly said she needed some space, so I came to hang out with Arran until she's asleep."

"What did you do?" Arran asks, sounding like he's ready to go to war on Tilly's behalf. Tilly has done so much for Starry Hill, it's no wonder he's feeling protective of his closest neighbor.

"She says I'm fussing too much." Bodin hardly moves his lips while speaking, but we can still make out the words.

"Are you?" I ask, fairly certain Tilly wouldn't kick him out for no reason.

"Maybe," Bodin admits with a heavy sigh.

When he doesn't elaborate, Arran asks, "Why?"

Bodin squares his shoulders and looks us in the eye. "Just trying to keep her safe. As always."

Sensing there's more to it, I ask, "Because of the baby?"

Arran swings his head toward Bodin. "The what?"

Bodin's eyes widen to saucers. "How did you know?"

I tap my nose. "You smell different. You always smell a little like Tilly, but her scent has shifted lately. It's sweeter." All pregnant creatures have a distinctly different scent, as if signaling to everyone that there is a baby within their womb. I'm sure I'm not the only one who has noticed this.

"You stopped drinking at game night," Arran remarks, slapping Bodin on the shoulder. "Congratulations. It's one of the signs of a good father, how you put the mother of your unborn child first with small actions."

Bodin rubs two hands down his face before clutching the back of his neck with both. "Fuck. I didn't realize it was that obvious. Tilly didn't want to tell anyone yet, but if you guys know, then I guess most of the island knows."

I nod and finally take a seat on Bodin's other side. "I'm certain they do."

For the first time, a smile pulls at the corner of Arran's mouth. "Like when we all pretended we didn't know you two were dating and fucking all over the island?"

Bodin huffs out a laugh. "Yeah, let's go back to pretending you don't know anything. At least until I've come up with a tactful way to convince Tilly to tell everyone soon."

Just when I thought our conversation was done and we can quietly enjoy the sound of waves crashing against the rock below, Arran asks me, "How's your dragon?"

"What do you mean?" Even though he's asleep, I can feel my dragon narrowing his eyes at me.

Arran rolls the die between his fingers, focusing on the motion as he speaks instead of the shiver of scales sweeping down my spine and along my arms. "I've noticed your dragon has made himself more apparent as of late. Especially when you mention Eleanor. I know you're not always in agreement with him, so I'm curious as to what your relationship is like these days."

I sigh and hold out my arm, watching my scales shimmer in the full moon's silvery light. "It's been getting harder to suppress him. He's been awake more often, especially when she's around, and wants to have his feelings heard too. Maybe I should look into getting a glamour ring so the scales won't be that noticeable?"

"No," Arran says, the word sharp and definitive. "Your dragon would hate that. You've suppressed him most of your life, bar the few times you give him the freedom to stretch his legs in the ocean. Pushing him down when he's trying harder to be heard would put you at even greater odds."

Now fully awake, my dragon raises his head to follow the conversation. "So, what? I should just embrace him and walk around with scales all the time? What if my horns appear too?"

I flash back to waking up in bed as a child, covered in scales, long horns protruding from my head, as my screams summon my grandmother to find me wholly transformed. It's a memory that hasn't surfaced in many years, but since Eleanor's been back, it haunts me often. She deserves to know the whole story, no matter how painful it is for me to relive it.

Unaware of the current turmoil in my head, Bodin offers gently, "Horns aren't the worst thing in the world." The thought makes me think of Ren and how cool his horns look. Maisie doesn't seem to mind them. Could I hope that Eleanor would accept mine too?

"Does your dragon like Eleanor?" Arran asks, his brows furrowed contemplatively.

I take a deep breath and let it out slowly. "Yeah, he really does. He's been more communicative with his feelings lately. My scales appear anytime we're worried or happy about anything related to her."

Bodin clasps a hand on my shoulder. "Beck, do you like Eleanor? Like 'big romantic feelings' like her?"

This time, the answer comes easily, and with it, a hefty boulder falls off my shoulders and rolls into the sea. "Yeah, I do." It's oddly liberating to share with my friends feelings I've been wrestling alone with for some time. "It started out as reconnecting as friends. I didn't expect anything more to develop, but my feelings have been slowly building with each afternoon spent together, each boat ride, each phone call." My mouth tugs up at the corners as I hold my hands out to describe the analogy that's playing in my mind. "It's like our friendship when we were kids was a tiny foundation, but as adults we've built on to that, one brick of conversation at a time. The walls around us are growing strong, and lately, we've added windows too. But I want more. I want a roof. A home. A relationship. I want Eleanor to be mine."

Arran clasps his hands together and stands up, turning toward us with more animation in his eyes than I've witnessed from him until now. "You know what you need to do? You need to enter into a courtship with this girl if you'd like to win her heart. Prove to Eleanor that you're worthy of her affection."

Confused, I glance at Bodin who looks rather entertained. "Courtship?"

"Aye," Arran states confidently. "It shows intention and requires thoughtful planning and consideration designed for your female in particular. I've seen it work. Most of the time."

Liking the sound of that, I lean forward and ask, "How do I do that?"

Bodin rubs his hands together eagerly as he stands up. "I can give you a couple of tips about things that worked for me. Though if all of us put our heads together, we can come up with a foolproof plan. But let's do that in the morning. I need to go home and check on my pregnant wife. Fuck, that feels good to say out loud." Heading away from us at a brisk jog, Bodin calls over his shoulder, "Let's meet at Ren's cottage after breakfast. I know he'll have some really good ideas too."

ELEANOR

CHAPTER 10

I pull into my apartment parking lot, turn off my car's engine, and stare blankly ahead, my body frozen while I disassociate from yet another miserable day at work. Part of me wants to reverse back out and drive straight to Starry Hill, leave this city and my stressful job behind, and enjoy the peace of the island, the sunshine, the books, the creatures... Beck.

But I remain frozen. There's no need to make my unhappiness anyone else's problem.

Eventually, I'll get out of this car. I'll head upstairs, pretend the day didn't happen, and go back tomorrow just to repeat it all again. And I'll keep doing that for as long as I need, because somehow when the gods were handing out courage, they skipped me.

As a young girl, I was promised that if I work hard and don't draw too much attention to myself, then I'll be rewarded with the respect of my peers. That's what my mother repeated to me over and over again as she straightened my curly hair before school every morning and tamed it into an inoffensive ponytail or bun that won't distract anyone else in my class. The same way I still wear it most days.

Except for when I go to Starry Hill. The rules feel different there. I'm not quite brave enough to try wearing my hair curly yet, but I've gotten as far as leaving it down. I've also splurged on a couple of pretty dresses for the weekends, clothes that actually make me happy each time I put them on, as opposed to the boxy blouses I wear to work.

Tap. Tap. Tap.

I scream as a face appears next to my window, my hand flying to my chest in an attempt to contain my racing heart from scuttling down to the footwell where it so desperately wants to go.

"Sorry," Audrey says with a slight cringe, lowering her sunglasses to see the apology in her eyes. "Didn't mean to scare you."

I'm already shaking my head as I lower my window, my heart now trying to return to a healthy human rhythm. "No, no. Not your fault. I guess I should be more observant. Sorry for screaming in your face."

"Honestly, it was a pretty good one," Audrey says, giving me a cheeky wink. "Before I make an inappropriate comment about situations that can elicit more screams from you, want to tell me what's on your mind? You've been sitting here for quite a while."

"I'm okay." The lie comes easily, the response fine-tuned with years of practice.

Audrey raises a single brow. "Work, family, boys, or all of the above?"

"Work." I let out a slow breath and, after another moment's hesitation, add, "Maybe a little bit of everything."

"Want to come upstairs and tell me about it?" Before I can refuse and tell Audrey I won't be great company, she says the magic words, "I have wine."

Audrey and I settle onto her couch in the living room with dinner ordered from the cute pasta place we both like, substantial wine glasses in hand.

Taking a big sip, Audrey eyes me over the rim of her glass. "Was it just a shitty day, or is there more to it?"

I puff out my cheeks while I contemplate my answer. "Today was especially shitty, but I'm starting to realize just how much I hate my job. Every day is a struggle to get through. It's like I'm living for the weekends. That's the only thing that keeps me sane at this point."

Audrey taps a dark nail against her glass as a sly grin plays on her lips. "I don't know how much help I can be on the work front, unless you want me to teach you some malicious compliance techniques that'll drive whoever's bothering you absolutely nuts."

"I couldn't."

"But if you change your mind, you know where to find me," Audrey says, twirling some pasta around her fork.

"I do. Thank you," I say around a mouthful of creamy goodness. "You're my favorite shit-stirrer I've ever met." It's not like I've met a ton of people as mischievous as Audrey, but even if I had, I'm sure she'd still be at the top of the list.

"A title I'll wear with pride." Crossing her legs, Audrey leans back on the couch and swirls her wine around as she contemplates something. "Maybe I can get a badge made. Or a sash. Next ladies' night on the island, I'll wear it."

I stare at my upstairs neighbor as a feeling of such gratefulness wraps around my heart. "I'm so happy our paths crossed."

"Me too. Now, tell me more about your weekends. What exactly is it about them that has you giddy enough to balance out your struggles? Or is it a who?"

Warmth spreads across my cheeks as numerous versions of Beck flash through my mind, each part etched onto my brain for different reasons. The way his whole body relaxes when his hand dips into the ocean, his genuine joy when we've made new plans together, the wide set of his shoulders when he's comfortably sprawled back in his seat, the way his voice gets all deep and rumbly on the phone when it's getting late, and the way his fingertips felt when they brushed against my cheek.

"Holy fucking hells, Eleanor. Who is it?" Audrey asks, setting down her wine like she's not willing to let her favorite adult beverage stand in the way of getting the whole story. I am the sole focus of her attention now, something that makes me want to both crawl into a hole but also revel in the momentary spotlight.

A thousand tiny wings flutter in my stomach and my heartbeat climbs into my throat. Am I finally going to tell someone? Will it make it more real if I say it aloud?

Unable to deny my feelings anymore, I let the butterflies in my stomach carry his name up until it whispers across my lips. "Beck."

"I fucking knew it. He's such a hottie. Well done you," Audrey says, holding up her hand for a high five.

Shaking my head profusely, I quickly lower her outstretched hand. "Oh no. We're just friends. But..."

"But what? Give me the juicy details," Audrey says, shifting forward to refill my glass before topping up her own.

I can't quite look at her as I admit, "I sometimes wish we could be more. He calls me almost every night, and we literally talk for hours. I'm even reading less these days because I'm enjoying talking to him more. That's never happened with anyone before."

"So what's holding you back from jumping his bones?"

"I'm not sure if he sees me as anything more than a friend." It's one of the biggest factors for keeping my guard up as high as I can with Beck, because having all of these feelings and finding out they're one-sided would be the most excruciating thing to ever happen to my heart. More so than finding my best friend gone the morning I was planning to ask him to be my first kiss.

Audrey sets her glass down so hard, a bit of wine spills over the side but she pays it no mind, concentrating all of her incredulity on me. "What the fuck are you talking about? No guy is willingly spending all night talking to a girl if he doesn't either really like her, or wants to fuck her. Or both."

I'm quick to counter that so-called fact. "But we used to talk like this when we were kids and—"

"I'm going to stop you right there," Audrey says, effectively cutting me off with a raised hand. "I know you guys were friends as kids, but you're not the same people you were then. You've got to think of this current version of who Beck is and who you are. Meet each other where you are at *this* point in time and stop trying to compare things to when you were kids. That's borderline gross."

I giggle at the disgust on her face and a tiny part of me thinks there might be a kernel of truth in what she's saying. "That's actually really good advice. Thank you."

Audrey picks up her wine again as another one of her signature smirks pulls at one corner of her mouth, making me nervous about what she's about to say. "If you want to test the waters, pun intended for your dragon boy, and see if he's ready to make a move, you can always just show him your spectacular tits."

"How do I—? How can—? No," I splutter, instinctively wrapping an arm across my large breasts.

Shrugging, Audrey gestures at my entire body with her glass. "If you're not going to show him your tits, then at least give him some kind of sign. That guy wouldn't get subtle hints. Write it on your forehead. Fall strategically face-first into his crotch, or sit on his hand, preferably when two fingers are facing up. And make sure you're shaved. Just in case," she adds with a wink.

"I'm not trying to fuck him."

"Ever?"

"I'm not saying that," I mumble, my cheeks burning with the admission. Just this past week I was searching again for any articles I could've missed on dragon anatomy. The results are still inconclusive, but some sites suggested that he might have two... appendages. I can't imagine that to be true, and knowing how secretive dragons are with their lore, I don't believe these claims are substantiated. But if Beck were to have feelings for me too, and he did happen to have two dicks, I'd certainly be up to the intriguing challenge. Though, I might need some prep work before I could take both.

Fuck, Eleanor. You're jumping ahead here. Figure out if he likes you first before you start contemplating double penetration.

Unaware of the naughty trajectory of my thoughts, Audrey stuffs another bite of pasta into her mouth before making a rather sage suggestion while pointing her fork at me. "Well, at least try to move things in that direction before you're stuck in the friendzone. That's a hard place to get out of."

"But isn't the friendzone better than no zone?" This is the question I've been battling with since I've realized my feelings have developed further than the mere platonic connection I thought we had.

Do I have moments imagining walking up to Beck, grabbing him by the shirt collar and pulling his mouth down to meet mine? Or perhaps pushing him down on the dock, straddling his hips right there instead of getting on the boat another Saturday evening? Maybe. But do I dare do anything as outrageous as that and risk our friendship? Honestly, no. Maybe if I had an iota of Audrey's courage, or Maisie's, or Tilly's. But my pusillanimous self could never.

Audrey leans forward and takes my hand, her smirk firmly packed away as she meets my eyes with a tenderness I rarely see from her. "If you really think you'd be okay to keep things the way they are now for the rest of your lives, then sure, staying in the friendzone is fine and dandy. However, if you have the opportunity to influence your own fate, maybe nudge it in a direction you think could make you happier than you are now, then I say grab it by the balls, twist it, and go for it."

"Nudge fate a little?" I ask, mulling the sound of that over in my head.

"Yeah."

"I think I can try a subtle nudge," I say, feeling a little bit of steel strengthen my spine as a smidgen of hope blooms in my chest.

"Good," Audrey says approvingly, a sneaky grin creeping back into place. "Then later Beck can nudge you with his dick."

A raucous burst of laughter bubbles out of me and I don't even try to hide how much I like the sound of that. Now I just need to manage getting through the week so I can try out my mediocre nudging skills on Saturday.

CHAPTER 11

I sense Eleanor as I make my way up Starry Hill, her fragrant lavender and sparkling water scent beckoning me closer to The Dancing Daisy. My dragon sniffs the air with me and scales shimmer down my spine as he urges me forward with extra enthusiasm.

Since I finally admitted to my friends, and myself, how much I like Eleanor, and acknowledged how much I want to be more than just her friend, it's like some type of barrier has been unlocked between my dragon and me. This week we've been more in tune with each other than usual, both of us now very keen on showing Eleanor how much we care for her, and ready to cautiously court her in the hopes that she'll accept our affection.

Cocking my head to the side, I pick up the conversation in the bookshop, my elevated hearing helping me get a picture of Eleanor and Lucille as I turn onto Third Street. I don't mean to blatantly eavesdrop, but I also don't make any effort to hasten my steps.

"Are you ready to host your first book club meeting next week?" Lucille asks Eleanor, the question sounding warm and encouraging, just as one might expect from Lucille.

Slowing down even further, I listen to Eleanor's response, enjoying the way I can hear her smile as she talks. "Yeah, I think we're all set. Marisol said she'll leave the door unlocked so I can get those extra chairs from The Singing Seahorse next door bright and early. I know we have only five confirmations, but I'll put out a couple more chairs just in case any latecomers want to join too." I frown at that. Eleanor has put so much effort into choosing a book, creating flyers that she personally delivered to each shop, coming up with discussion questions... Having only five creatures confirm their attendance is unfair to her. I don't want Eleanor to be discouraged by a lackluster response.

Before I can figure out how I can fix this, Eleanor continues, "Maisie is delivering our themed cupcakes around nine, which reminds me that I need to ask Beck if he'd be willing to pick me up a little earlier so I can get everything set up."

"Eleanor, I think Beck is willing to do pretty much anything for you," Lucille says wisely, understanding my feelings for Eleanor better than I thought she did.

"I doubt that, but even if he were, I'd never want to take advantage of him," Eleanor protests.

Take advantage. Please, I want to say. Instead, I keep my lips pressed together as I mentally reschedule next week's supply run and ferry times while stomping on the cobbled street so the women can hear me approaching.

Seeing Eleanor's face brighten, her smile wide and eyes sparkling the moment she spots me in the doorway, sends scales fluttering across my cheeks and down my chest, before they dissipate somewhere above my cocks. It's the same expression she has when I show up in Cape Easton every Saturday, and it never fails to call forth my own smile, to make my stomach feel swoopy, and to get my dragon's attention.

Eleanor walks toward me, but stops short an arm's length away, her expression flitting between happy and... concerned? "Hi. Is everything okay?"

My first instinct is to say no, because how could it be when she's standing so close when I'm aching to wrap my arms around her but can't? And today especially, when she looks extra beautiful in an aquamarine dress that makes her hair look even brighter, more stunning.

"Yes. Why wouldn't it be?" I ask, pretending I'm not salivating for her.

Eleanor quickly scans my body before her gaze settles on my eyes. "I always meet you at your mill after I'm finished. Did something happen? Or am I late?" Eleanor's pillowy lips that are normally turned up at the corners, are pulled down with worry. Everything within me begs to lean forward, place the gentlest of kisses to each corner of her mouth before pressing my lips to hers, parting them with my tongue, and finally finding out what she tastes like.

I try to redirect my attention from her lips and actually focus on the words she's saying, but my brain feels slow to respond now that I've given myself free rein to truly appreciate all of Eleanor's alluring qualities. "Oh, no. Everything's fine. I—" I didn't foresee Eleanor misunderstanding why I showed up here instead of waiting for her at home, like I usually do. Coming to the bookshop is supposed to be part of my courting tactics, but what if I'm bothering her?

My throat constricts and an uncomfortable warmth climbs up my neck and burns the tips of my ears. "I was done early with all my duties so I thought I'd walk back with you. When you're done, of course," I add hastily. "No need to rush. Or maybe there's something here I can help with?"

I follow Eleanor's gaze as she looks behind her, but Lucille has disappeared into the back room on feet way more silent than I thought was possible for a human.

Tucking her hair behind her ear, Eleanor looks up at me with a smile that seems satisfied with my explanation. "That's very kind of you. Thank you, Beck."

Lucille appears from the back, shuffling between the shelves toward us, holding Eleanor's bag out for her while giving me an approving nod. "Hi, dear boy. We were just wrapping up." Patting Eleanor's hand, Lucille says, "I've put a bag of those candies you've been wanting to try in your tote. They're always more fun when enjoyed with someone else. Now off you go, and have fun. See you next weekend."

Eleanor says a quick goodbye and I incline my head toward Lucille as she winks at me with a secretive grin.

"Have you eaten yet?" I ask Eleanor as we make our way down the hill.

"Not yet," she admits, sounding a little confused, and still unaware that I planned for this. "Richard usually brings us some of their specials from The Flowering Teapot around lunch time, but I guess they've been quite busy today?"

"Good."

"Good?"

I clear my throat and try not to sound too pleased with myself that everything's going according to plan so far. "Yeah, because now we can have lunch together. I've been experimenting with a new sourdough recipe all week and I finally feel happy with the flavors."

Eleanor lays a hand on my arm, her touch sending a thrill right through my body, my cocks responding as eagerly as the scales flitting down my abdomen. "That's really nice of you to offer, but aren't you saving it for the boys tonight?"

"Uhm, boys' night got cancelled. Unfortunately." The words stumble clumsily out of my mouth and a light sense of panic threatens to take root. I'm such a bad liar and I didn't plan on Eleanor being this concerned.

"Oh no. Is everything okay?" Eleanor asks, her hand lightly squeezing my forearm, anchoring me to her in a way I'd never tire of.

I bend my arm to encourage her hand to stay on me, and Eleanor obliges, slipping her hand into my crook like it's the most natural thing to do. I try to breathe normally, but having her skin against mine makes it hard to simply remember what day of the week it is.

Realizing the guys and I didn't think of a believable excuse for canceling game night so I can court Eleanor, I blurt out the first thing that comes to mind. "Tilly is angry at Bodin, so he wants to do something nice for her. A date. We thought it best to postpone tonight's session, for the sake of their marriage."

"Really? I'm sorry to hear that. Tilly didn't seem upset when I saw her at the shop this morning, quite the opposite actually. She was practically glowing. But maybe she was masking. So many of us do that. I hope they'll be okay. They're such a lovely couple."

"They will be. Bodin is a good guy," I state, knowing that's the truth, even if they're not really fighting.

"I know he is," Eleanor agrees, grazing her thumb across my forearm, my dragon practically purring in my chest at all the contact. "But it's also good that he's prioritizing his wife."

Meeting Eleanor's honey-brown eyes, I lay my hand on top of hers as her heart goes into a gallop. "Yes. Putting your partner first is the epitome of a good relationship."

Our hands remain like that for the rest of the walk home. Being with Eleanor is easy and exhilarating at the same time, making my nerves compete with excitement for the rest of our first unofficial date.

"It smells great in here. What flavors did you use?" Eleanor asks as I open the mill's front door for her.

Inhaling deeply as she steps past me, I close my eyes and let her scent wash through me, savoring the way it blends so seamlessly with the other familiar smells in my home. When I open my eyes again, I give myself a moment to enjoy the sight of Eleanor in my space. I've always appreciated how beautiful she is, but being more in touch with my actual feelings now, I can acknowledge that I've wanted her since the first second I saw her again. It was just too scary to allow myself to hope for anything more, so I suppressed my attraction, much to my dragon's dislike too.

But now, watching Eleanor stand in the center of my kitchen with the sunlight beaming down on her like a personal spotlight, highlighting every one of her curves like the goddess she is, makes me believe fate has brought her back to me for a reason.

I lick my lips, imagining undoing the thin little bows on her shoulders and slipping off that pretty aquamarine dress until it pools at her feet. I want to fall down on my knees and kiss every inch of her silky skin, working my way up, then bury my face in her sweet cunt. Because Eleanor is a woman meant to be worshipped.

"Beck?" Eleanor asks in a way that makes me think it might not be the first time she's tried to get my attention.

I ignore the scales now flickering all over my body, most of them congregating around my cocks, and shake my head to clear the wanton thoughts, knowing it's not the time for that yet. Courting first. "Sorry, my mind was somewhere else. What was the question?"

Eleanor purses her lips together, but her smile still manages to sneak through. "The flavors? I was wondering what bread it is. I think I'm getting hints of cinnamon?"

Suddenly feeling awkward and not knowing what to do with my limbs, I brush my hair back before putting both hands in my pockets. "The first time you brought me bread, you said you couldn't choose your favorite, so you got me both. Well, I combined them into one sourdough loaf—cranberry, orange, walnut, and cinnamon. I've been practicing different ratios and combinations all week, but I think I've finally found a good balance that you'll like."

Eleanor's mouth opens slowly, her eyes flitting in a triangle across my face as her heart speeds up. It's not beating the same as it does when she gets on the boat, and I can't smell her nerves, but I understand it's still inappropriate to ask her what this emotion is.

With one hand on her chest, Eleanor walks toward me, her heart beating faster and faster. "That's... wow. So much effort, and planning, and— You're really thoughtful, Beck. Clever, and kind." Her arms wrap around my waist as she hugs me. "Thank you."

Feeling Eleanor's body pressed to mine for the first time is better than I could have dreamed, and I never want it to stop. Soft curves mold to my harder lines, as her head settles against my solar plexus. Stunned, I realize almost too late that my hands are still in my pockets, so I quickly take them out and fold my arms around her before she can retreat without my returned affection. We stay wrapped together for a couple of seconds, my breathing shallow as I try to keep myself from tracing a hand up to her nape, tilting her head back, and kissing her the way I want to so badly.

Eventually, I make the smarter choice to step back, even if I'm unable to fully let go of her. Keeping a hand on Eleanor's shoulder, I whisper, "You're very welcome." My eyes dip to her mouth for a prolonged moment before I'm able to snap my lustful intentions away. Letting my hand skim down Eleanor's arm, I enjoy the sight of goose bumps appearing in the wake of my touch, then I take her hand and lead her to the table where there's a variety of spreads around the covered bread.

Feeling unsure of what to do next, I flounder with the assortment of toppings Maisie suggested when she sat in on the courting meeting at her and Ren's cottage.

So far, this date is going pretty smoothly, much better than I expected, but I'm scared I might be moving too fast and getting ahead of myself. What if Eleanor isn't ready for my advances? I need to slow down before I say or do something she's not ready for.

"Can I help?" Eleanor asks.

"No. Thank you. You're my guest. Just sit back and relax," I say while wrestling the lid off a jar of orange marmalade.

"I hope I'm more than a guest by now." The words are hesitant, yet there's a hint of playfulness woven into them, and I don't know how to interpret that.

Pausing with a container of hummus in my hand, I study Eleanor's face. "Yeah?"

"Uhm, I mean, I'm here every Saturday afternoon. It's about time I make myself more useful," Eleanor explains, putting things in a little more perspective for me. For a moment I thought she meant it in a romantic way. Glad I asked her to clarify before my heart jumped to conclusions.

"Oh." I take the seat next to Eleanor and place a plate in front of her. "You can help by fixing yourself a plate. You must be really hungry by now and that's never good for anyone."

Eleanor smiles to herself as she studies the assortment, lifting jars to read their labels. "Thank you for going through all the trouble of putting this together. For baking the bread, and preparing everything. Just look at all these spreads. There is quite literally nowhere else in the world I'd rather be today than right here, with you." The last two words are barely a breath, but my dragon hears them, sending a cascade of scales raining down my body while he stretches out on his back with a smirk of contentment.

"Me too," I whisper back, feeling like the luckiest creature in the world.

ELEANOR

CHAPTER 12

As the sun stretches toward the western horizon, a pang of melancholy threatens my mood, but it quickly dissipates when I remember there's no need to rush back to the city tonight. I get to stay and finally enjoy my first full sunset on Starry Hill. With Beck.

He's been acting differently all day, more attentive, and way more tactile than usual, which leads me to believe there could be some truth to Audrey's theory. Maybe Beck does like me a little bit too? I don't want to get my hopes up yet, but so far I'm enjoying every extra brush of skin, each new touch sending a spark racing through my body.

"Since I don't have to leave early tonight, do you want to go sit on the dock and watch the sunset with me?" I ask, feeling like a shy girl asking out the most handsome boy at school. Despite being a lawyer who leads meetings, there are times—like now—where I still feel like the awkward teenager I once was.

"Yes," Beck answers without a beat of hesitation, effectively stopping my insecurities in their tracks. "Let's take that bag of candies from Lucille with us."

"Good idea. I've been asking her about them, but I haven't been brave enough to try one yet," I say, heading over to the couch to get Lucille's bag of colorful treats from my tote.

Beck leans against the doorframe as he watches me, and I try not to drool at the way his arms look crossed over his chest. But it's so hard when he's this pretty and he's right in front of me.

"Maybe I can hold your hand and help you be brave?" Beck suggests around a swallow, his pale ocean eyes never leaving me for a second.

My heart kicks into overdrive and a frenzied rabble of butterflies takes flight in my stomach. That might be the most forward thing Beck's said to me yet. The tiny bead of hope in my chest billows into a fluffy cloud that just about has me levitating off the floor.

Stopping in front of Beck, I lightly poke him on the chest, enjoying the hard muscles way too much. "You might be teasing me, but I'm definitely taking you up on that offer."

Beck closes his fingers around mine, pressing my hand to his chest. Underneath my palm, his heart also races, its rhythm an echo to mine as our gazes lock. My breathing speeds up and

Beck's eyes dip to my mouth, then to my chest, before leisurely making their way up again.

I'm lightheaded, my whole body tingling with anticipation. *Is he going to kiss me?!*

Beautiful opalescent scales scuttle down his neck, disappearing underneath his shirt where I can feel the smooth, overlapping texture against my fingertips. Beck gives me the smallest of smiles and, still holding my hand, wordlessly leads me outside to the waiting blue and orange skies.

When we get to the dock, we kick off our shoes, our feet padding lightly across the sturdy timber as we walk all the way to the end. In the distance, the ocean mirrors the sky, fiery oranges and pinks and purples blend together on the horizon, creating the most serene view my eyes have ever had the pleasure to witness.

Beck helps me down onto the edge of the dock and waits for me to get comfortable before sitting down next to me, our sides brushing against each other, our hands clasped, as our legs dangle above the gently undulating water.

I breathe in the serenity of the moment, wanting to take a mental snapshot with all my senses that'll be embedded in my brain forever. The way molten pools of sunlight gather between calm ripples, the amiable whispers of waves lapping against the shore, and the steadfast presence of Beck at my side.

"Do you know how much it sucks to always leave right when Starry Hill is at its prettiest?" I ask when I finally find my ability to speak again.

"You don't have to leave." The words are so soft, I swear I imagined them, but the pink spreading across Beck's cheeks makes me think they're real. Before I have time to ask him what he means by that, he reaches for the candy bag. "Do you want me to tell you what each one is, or do you want to be surprised?"

"Maybe a little bit of both? Give me a hint of what they can do, but don't tell me which is which. That way I have some context and can still be surprised."

"Sure," Beck says, opening the paper bag and glancing at its contents. "Lucille probably explained it to you, but each candy's effect only lasts one minute maximum, so you don't have to worry that you'll be stuck like that forever."

"She did mention that, but it's good to be reminded. Can you imagine my lips turning green and thinking I'll have to walk into my Monday morning briefing like that?" I say, a shudder rolling down my spine at the mere thought of work and the reactions that look would elicit.

Beck rubs his thumb across the back of my hand, the sweet gesture quickly bringing me back to the present. "There's nothing scary in here, but even if there was, you're always safe with me."

"I know."

Our eyes meet and hold, the truth of his statement feeling like a promise burrowing into my heart.

A lock of hair falls free from Beck's hair tie as he looks down at me, and shoving away my self-doubt, I slowly reach up with my free hand and tuck the silky strands behind his ear. My hand lingers there for a moment, enjoying the way Beck leans into my touch, before I finally lower it back into my lap.

Beck remains frozen for a few seconds, then he offers the bag to me as he explains, "So, you've got giggling candy, lip candy, hair candy, prank candy, growing candy, and truth candy."

"Truth candy? I don't think I remember Lucille mentioning that one."

"I think it's a new addition," Beck says, looking a little embarrassed. "But we can skip it if it makes you uncomfortable?"

"No, it's good. What's a little bit of truth between friends?" The moment that *F* word is out of my mouth, I want to jump into the ether and bring it back. Things were going so well, we're literally sitting here holding hands at sunset, and now it sounds like I'm trying to friendzone him. What the fuck is wrong with me?

Unaware of my mental meltdown and mortification, Beck squeezes my hand as a little bit of excitement dances in his eyes. "The truth will set us free."

Thinking there might be something to that, I ask, "Are there two of each? Like, can we both have one at the same time and get the same effect?"

"Yes. That's exactly what Lucille packed in here. She must've thought ahead. We'll do each one together."

"Together." This word sounds much better and not friendzony at all. I reach into the bag and grab two of the squishy purple candies. "Ready?"

"Good choice for our first one." Beck takes his purple candy from my open palm, and we bump them together in a toast before popping them in our mouths at the same time.

It tastes like a normal sweet candy, but soon little tingles erupt along my scalp. I forget to look at my own hair as I stare up at Beck, his silvery-blond hair transforming into a chocolate-brown hue right in front of my eyes.

His upper lip curls back as his gaze flits all over me. "No. No, no, no. Please never dye your hair black."

"Oh?" I scoop my hair forward over my shoulder and look at the midnight strands against my skin, kind of seeing his point. "It looks bad, doesn't it?"

Beck's entire face softens and he shakes his head. "I don't think you can look bad if you tried, but I love the vibrant copper of your real hair. It looks like a fiery crown. It suits you much better than this black color."

"Thank you. That means a lot to me. Brown looks good on you, though."

The next candy we try is an orange triangle that has us giggling for a minute straight, my cheeks aching happily as I fall into Beck's side. After that, the growing candy enlarges Beck's feet a significant couple of sizes, while I add a few inches to my height. I stand up to walk around with my longer legs, wanting to experience the world from a higher point of view for a minute, before I sit down again and giggle at Beck's clown feet.

Beck hands me a jelly swirl next, which I recognize as the lip candy I've wanted to try. We take them at the same time, and I watch transfixed as Beck's lips transform into a blue pout. Slowly, he lifts his hand and reaches forward.

"This magenta color suits you, but then again, anything does," Beck whispers as his thumb grazes along my bottom lip.

My mouth parts and I hold absolutely still as he traces the outline of my mouth with a featherlight touch. His eyes flick up to mine, and when I see the raw desire in his gaze, my breath catches.

Every hint of apprehension, every thread of doubt I had about our feelings for each other blows away on the next gust of wind.

Feeling brave, I say, "Let's have those truth candies now."

"Okay." Confusion furrows Beck's brow, but he follows my request and holds out the unassuming white star-shaped candies in his hand.

Our eyes stay locked as we chew on the sweet confection, and in my peripheral vision the sun melts into the ocean, the entire moment feeling suspended somewhere between a dream and reality.

Light flutters through my veins and a goofy grin pulls at my mouth. "Ask me, Beck."

"Anything?"

"Anything."

Beck's tongue darts out to wet his lips. "Eleanor, can I kiss you?"

"I'd like nothing more."

Gentle fingers lift my hand toward his mouth, and Beck presses his lips to my knuckles, working his way across my whole hand. My heart rate ratchets up as he turns my hand over and kisses the inside of my palm before grazing his nose along the sensitive skin and brushing his lips against my wrist, goose bumps scattering up my arm and down my spine as my breathing turns shallow.

Beck places my hand on his chest, right on top of his racing heart, as he cups my jaw, his eyes once more checking in with me before they lock on my lips.

"I've been wanting to do this," Beck whispers as he lowers his head slowly and places the lightest of kisses on the corner of my mouth.

A breathy sound escapes me as I sink into his touch, my mouth parting for more. But Beck takes his time, savoring this moment, savoring me, like this is the most important kiss of his life and he doesn't want it over anytime soon.

Beck presses another kiss to the other corner of my mouth, then meets my eyes again. I give him a small nod and rub my thumb across the hard scales forming under my touch, reassuring him I'm still very much consenting to all of his affection.

Reality ceases to exist as Beck finally brushes his mouth against mine.

The first caress of our lips is tentative, like we're both almost unable to believe this is really happening. But the moment our tongues meet, a fire is lit within me and I never want it gone.

Everything about this kiss feels different, everything with Beck feels different, and all that I am wants to guard this special connection, keep it safe, and make it last.

Beck's fingers tighten on me, moving to my nape as he draws me closer. My arms go around his neck as our kiss grows stronger, our tongues tasting, dancing, playing.

Then, I'm in Beck's lap. He lifts me up and my knees land on both sides of his hips, and his arms wrap around me to keep me secure in his embrace as our kiss grows hungrier.

Just before I start writhing on his lap and think about taking this further, Beck slows our kiss down and rests our foreheads together.

"Eleanor?" Beck says, his breathlessness holding awe.

"Beck?" I ask, leaning back only far enough to take in his incredulous grin that pretty much mirrors mine.

"I have a confession to make." There's no guilt or maliciousness in the statement, so my walls remain down as his fingers rub up and down my back.

"Yeah?" I encourage, twirling a strand of his pretty hair around my finger.

Beck ducks his head to meet my eyes. "I know I said I wanted to be friends again. I lied. I want more than that."

"Me too. So much more."

"And, there's one more thing," Beck adds, shoulders climbing up toward his ears.

"Yeah?" Apprehension threatens my good mood, but once again, I aim to give him the benefit of the doubt.

"Tilly and Bodin aren't fighting. I made that up as an excuse to spend more time with you. The guys helped me plan everything for today and postponed game night," Beck admits, imploring me to understand with the most beautiful puppy eyes I'm increasingly weak for.

My smile grows slowly, enjoying the effort he's put into this day and the fact that he enlisted his friends for some help. For *me*. "That's actually really endearing. I love the team effort."

Beck's brow furrows and his mouth sets in a serious line. "Eleanor, more than a minute has passed since we've had the truth candies, so I'm saying all of this without any coercion. I want you to know that I won't lie to you again. Ever."

Whispering fingers across his brow and down the scales along his jaw, I say, "I'll always tell you the truth, too. Promise."

"Promise," Beck echoes before sealing our vow with a kiss.

BECK

CHAPTER 13

After a super busy Friday, I fall onto my couch, checking my phone's battery for the umpteenth time before glancing at the clock too. I rub at the scales on my chest, right above the spot where my dragon sits, waiting patiently to hear Eleanor's voice soon.

This week has been like no other for many reasons. Eleanor being the main one, but a close second is the improvement in my relationship with my dragon. I've gone for a swim every morning, easily shifting into my dragon form and allowing him to guide me where he wants us to go. Not constantly suppressing him turns out to be very good for both of us, especially when it comes to the affection we both share for Eleanor.

Another highlight has been that my friends had made time to come and visit me at my mill. It started with them asking about how the date went, but each felt compelled to give me advice on what they think I should do next. I appreciate their input, but their ideas are all so different that it makes my head spin. Not all of us have the confidence of Bodin to throw a woman over his shoulder and fuck her on a table in the garden. Or have a picnic in a pretty location, like Ren suggested, only to turn that too into some kind of foreplay.

Though, I certainly won't mind having more opportunities to touch Eleanor, to kiss her, taste her. I want to find out what sounds she makes when she's at the height of pleasure. I want to watch her face when she surrenders, knowing it's me who's got her safe in his arms. But not yet. Above all, I don't want to rush things with Eleanor. I've waited twenty-two years to see her again and I will not risk fucking things up... again.

Surprisingly, Arran had the best advice of all: Find out what Eleanor likes, and do more of that.

I know she likes books, bread, wine, Starry Hill, and phone calls with me. I aim to give her all of that, and more, whenever she's ready.

So far, I've rescheduled my supply runs and consulted Viggo to do ferry runs this Saturday so I can be free to attend Eleanor's book club. Every spare second I've had this week was used to finish reading the book she picked, clean my house, and practice a new recipe to bake for her.

Glancing down at my phone, my whole body ignites as Eleanor's name flashes on the screen. "Hello."

A second of heavy silence passes before Eleanor breathes out a shaky, "Hi, Beck."

Instantly, I'm on my feet, my dragon also on high alert. "What's wrong?"

"Nothing," Eleanor replies, but the lie is obvious. "I mean, nothing major is technically wrong. I just had a really shitty day, but I'm glad to hear your voice now."

My free hand shoots into my hair and tugs on the strands. "Where are you?"

"I don't want to tell you," Eleanor says. It's like I can hear a wince in her voice, but it's hard to pinpoint the emotion exactly. I need to see her to know she's okay.

"Why not?" I ask, staring out the window as if the ocean is going to give me some kind of answer.

Eleanor hesitates a beat. "Because you'll think I'm weird."

"Please tell me you're safe." My dragon paces up and down, my scales fluttering wildly all over my body as worry roils through us.

"I'm safe, I promise," Eleanor says quickly. "I just... I wanted to see the ocean today. I hoped some of that calm it brings you would rub off on me, so I drove to the harbor."

"Cape Easton harbor?"

"Yes."

"Are you hurt?"

"No."

"Are you alone?"

"Yes."

"Wait there."

Faster than I've ever run before, I sprint out of the house and toward my boat. I yank on the rope, quickly undo it from the cleats, and toss it into the water before stripping my clothes off and throwing them into the boat.

Then, I jump.

When it comes to Eleanor, my dragon and I are very much on the same page, so he doesn't need any further prodding to take over my body, shifting midair into our monstrous form so we can get to her as fast as possible.

Horns erupt from my head and my giant maw closes around the rope before I break the surface, pulling the boat behind me as I swim for Cape Easton. My long serpentine body undulates through the water, and I call on the ocean to speed me along, letting the current take me toward my girl.

My dragon and I are united, breathing as one, our thoughts and purpose aligned to protect one of our own. Even if we're technically only meant to protect Starry Hill, for us, Eleanor is part of that, and where she is, we'll go.

I duck below the surface, swimming faster and faster, not caring who can see me or who I can frighten as I focus on my sole priority—getting Eleanor safely in my arms.

It doesn't take long until Cape Easton comes into view and I slow only long enough to plot the shortest course through the different boats returning to the harbor.

When I get into shallow water, I shift back into my human form, jump into the boat, dry myself with my water magic, and pull on my clothes. I'm already scanning the car park in the distance for Eleanor's car while I loosely secure the boat.

Relief floods me as I spot Eleanor with her phone in her hand, staring at the device while absent-mindedly biting on a nail. Then, I'm sprinting toward her.

She must see me coming out of the corner of her eye, because her head turns toward me when I'm still a couple of yards away. The emotion on Eleanor's face flits between surprise, relief, and disbelief, but then she's opening her car door and walking straight into my waiting arms.

"You're here," Eleanor says, the words muffled against my chest.

"Of course." I refuse to entertain any other option than being there for her whenever she needs me. The painful memory of watching from my window as Eleanor waited for me, all alone in her backyard so many years ago, still haunts me. The day before I decided to court Eleanor, I vowed to myself that I won't be the reason for her tears ever again, and I aim to keep that promise until my dying breath.

"Are you okay?" I ask, tilting her head back to really study her face.

"I am now," Eleanor breathes out, lifting onto her toes and pulling me down toward her.

The kiss is sweet, soft, a gentle brushing of lips with only the slightest hint of our tongues meeting, and it speaks of the comfort of being reunited, saying so much more than I could put in words at the minute. I don't think I'll ever get used to the fact that I get to kiss Eleanor, a dream my teenage self didn't even have the courage to wish for.

Leaning back with her arms still wrapped around my waist, Eleanor asks, "How did you get here so fast?"

"I swam. In my dragon form," I admit, my eyes flitting over her face to gauge her reaction.

"I'd like to see him one day," Eleanor says, one finger tracing over the scales still visible in the V-neck of my shirt.

"Yeah?"

"Yeah. I bet he's cute," Eleanor says, the most adorable smile pulling at the corner of her mouth that I can't help but trace with my thumb.

Hearing those words, my dragon basically flutters his eyelashes, imploring me to show her soon.

"I don't know about cute, but he'll be happy you thought that," I say, trying to communicate on my dragon's behalf.

Eleanor reaches up to cup my face. "Thank you for coming. I would've been okay, but I feel much better now that I've seen you."

Folding my fingers around hers, I lean down and whisper, "Come back to Starry Hill with me."

"I can't," Eleanor whispers back with a slight shake of her head.

"Why not?"

"I came here straight from work," Eleanor says, gesturing to her formal office wear, as if that makes sense as an excuse. "Besides, if I go with you now then you'd have to bring me back later tonight and pick me up again tomorrow morning only to bring me back again in the evening. I refuse to be a burden for you."

"You couldn't be a burden if you tried," I say, cupping her face between both my hands. "But I mean, come stay the night with me. Nothing has to happen. It's just, I can't stand the thought of you being alone when you're upset."

"Should I go back home first and pack a—"

"No," I interrupt quickly before she starts to overthink things. If clothing is Eleanor's only reason to consider saying no, I'll find her ten other garments to wear. "We'll figure everything out. I promise."

Eleanor takes a second to respond, her eyes flicking between mine as a decision wars within her, then finally, a smile creeps across her face. Nodding, she breathes out, "Okay. Take me to Starry Hill."

Warmth floods my veins from head to toe before settling in my heart, expanding the organ at least five times its size before Eleanor came back into my life. Excitement and relief, nervousness and lust drum against each other, as Eleanor grabs her tote bag, locks her car, and walks with me hand in hand toward the dock.

Our steps are light, quick, bordering on giddy as we keep glancing at each other, smiling like two creatures setting off on an adventure.

As we near the boat, I note Eleanor's heart beating erratically, the same way it usually does before we set sail, and I glance over at her. "I don't know how to phrase this politely, but I can sense your nerves. Is it because of me, my boat, the ocean, or something else?"

"Full honest answer?"

"Please."

Eleanor sucks her lip into her mouth as she gathers her thoughts, then slowly explains, "You sometimes make me nervous, but in a good way. The thing is..." She lifts her thumb to her mouth as if to chew on it again, but decides against it at the last second, then continues haltingly, "It's not that your boat is bad or anything, it's just that it's a tiny vessel on a very large ocean. And well, I'm not particularly comfortable in the ocean. I usually like to remain on the shore and admire it from afar, somewhere I can adequately respect its vastness and the many, many unknown creatures it hides beneath the surface."

"But you're on top of the ocean. And with me," I argue, not really understanding her reasoning.

Stopping in front of my boat, Eleanor shrugs shyly as she stares at her feet. "Logically, I know nothing will attack me, and I know I probably won't fall out of the boat and be drowned by something, but the ocean is just *so* big and there are *so* many things we don't know about it."

I move closer to Eleanor and tilt her chin up. "Do you trust me?"

"Of course."

A little scared of what I'm about to confess, but needing her to understand who I really am, I square my shoulders and say, "I'm the scariest thing in the ocean. As long as you're with me, nothing will dare to come close to us. I'll always keep you safe. I promise."

"Really?"

"Really."

"That does make me feel better," Eleanor admits, trailing a finger up my chest until she can cup the back of my neck. She draws me down to her, then whispers against my lips, "My own protective dragon. I like the sound of that."

"Good," I whisper back before claiming her mouth with a fierce kiss, the tension of the last hour bleeding out of me with every second our lips are locked, and redirecting everything else to my hardening cocks.

I told Eleanor nothing has to happen tonight, and I truly meant it. But if she keeps kissing me like this while smelling so enticing, I might beg her to bury my face in her sweet, sweet cunt.

 ELEANOR

CHAPTER 14

Beck helps me into his boat and positions me between his legs with my back to his front. He wraps one arm around me, and places his other in the water, guiding us out of the harbor the same way he has on so many other occasions.

Only this time, everything feels better, easier, more significant as a thousand new possibilities blossom in my heart.

With my sailing nerves now the teensiest fraction of what they usually are, I relax into Beck's safe hold, his touch sending all other kinds of sensations through me as we unhurriedly make our way back to Starry Hill.

With the way Beck's been making me feel lately, I just want to strip him naked and have my way with him tonight. But it's much too soon for that, and exactly the reason I'll be offering to sleep on the couch. Beck is worth so much more than a single night of lust. He deserves all the good things in the world, and I really, really want to get everything right with him. I want us to take our time, to really settle into our new dynamic, savor it all, before I allow my pussy to wrestle control from my brain.

Yet, I feel like Beck deserves a reward for rescuing me from my gloomy mood and taking me away to the place I feel the happiest in the world. Perhaps later, if we happen to be cuddling on the couch, my hands could drift south, or my mouth could, but only if he explicitly consents.

As the sun dips below the horizon behind us, Beck places his mouth right by ear, his lips skimming against the sensitive flesh as he asks, "Do you want to feel my magic?"

I turn back to look at him, wondering if it's a euphemism for something sexy. "Your what?"

"My ocean magic. Here, give me your hand." Beck laces our fingers and scoops me into his lap to give me better reach before lowering our joint hands into the water.

I'm still debating if I should protest sitting on top of him, always feeling a little self-conscious of my weight, but then a flurry of bubbles dance around my hand, and a preposterous giggle escapes me at the wonder of it all.

"This is amazing," I exclaim, marveling at the sensation.

"Look at you enjoying the ocean," Beck jokes, and presses a quick kiss to my neck.

I honestly don't know if I should swoon or laugh, my body and brain still playing catch up with the curveball this evening has thrown at me. It's like I'm in a dream and I don't know what I did to deserve it.

One thing I do know is that I'm happy—full-heart, d a n c i n g - i n - t h e - m o o n l i g h t , quit-my-job-and-move-to-Starry-Hill-to-live-with-Beck-forever-and-ever levels of happy.

But somewhere in the back of my mind, my mother whispers her toxic words, *Happiness doesn't last forever, Eleanor. You need security. A good job with a good salary. The respect of your peers. All of that will lead to feelings of contentment that will sustain you much longer than the fleeting feeling of happiness.*

I mentally bat her away and focus on the sensation of Beck's hands intertwined with mine, his breath against my neck, and the comfort of his embrace, letting it all center me in the present. I want to live for *these* moments, build a catalog of happy memories I can flit through when I've had a shitty day, and find joy in all the small things.

For too long I believed my mother, for too long I followed her advice, thinking her way is the only way to live, hoping one day to truly make her proud of me. Now, I'm ready to shut the door on all these inaccurate beliefs, to follow my own definition of happiness, because this right here, this is it for me.

Turning my head, I slant my mouth against Beck's and kiss him with all the gratefulness I feel for him. I'm not sure if he fully understands what he's done for me. Not only does Beck make me feel seen, but he literally jumped to my rescue when he thought I needed him. I want him to feel just as special, as appreciated, as valued, as he makes me feel.

When we come up for air again, our boat is drifting somewhere in the middle of the ocean with no land in sight. For not even a second do I feel scared of being unmoored in the dark. Quite the opposite, in fact, as Beck presses soft, open-mouthed kisses along every inch of exposed skin he can reach while the stars blink down at us.

"So you can control water too?" I ask, aiming for a normal conversation, despite my husky voice betraying how turned on I still am.

"Yeah," Beck answers, lowering his hand back into the water to resume our journey. "My magic is why I've got the mill. It supplies hydropower to all the shops in the main part of town. That's where all the creatures used to live a long time ago, but as the population expanded, creatures needed more space, and the cottages were built around the island. We use generators for the homes because Arran doesn't want Starry Hill to become some type of modern, overcrowded city filled with cables and wires and such. He's not a fan of big changes."

"He's Starry Hill's founder, right?" I ask, lazily tracing the scales on his arm that haven't disappeared yet.

"Yes. He started building here about four hundred years ago, and has since given so many of us a place to call home when there weren't a variety of good options available to us." The pain in Beck's voice slices through me and I squeeze his hand a little tighter.

"I'd like to meet him sometime. You sound like you care for him," I say gently.

Beck's smile is wistful as the familiar outline of Starry Hill comes into view. "It's a long story, but Arran offered me the position of island guardian when I was in a fairly dark place. I owe him a lot. One day I'd like to tell you the whole story. Right now, though, I want to focus on making you happy and helping you forget the terrible day you had."

Part of me wants to ask Beck to tell me everything now. I want to understand his pain, and help him ease it. But if he's not ready, then I'm not going to push him. I just hope someday in the not-too-distant future he'll be comfortable enough to tell me all of it—why he disappeared when we were kids, how he ended up here, and why everything happened.

Pulling Beck's arm more snuggly around me, I say, "This right here, with you, this is happiness to me. There's nowhere else I'd rather be."

When we get to the mill, Beck takes out the dough that's been proving and prepares a spinach-and-artichoke filling for them. I watch, completely fascinated, as he moves around the rustic kitchen with complete ease.

Beck separates the dough into equal parts, wraps them around the filling before shaping them into perfect balls, and then pops the lot into the oven, all like it's no big deal. He's clearly unaware of how attractive it is to watch not only how comfortable he is in the kitchen, but also how good he is with his hands.

"I would say I'm sorry I didn't prepare any bread for you this week, but that would be a lie," I drawl, leaning back in my chair to properly appreciate the view of Beck bending down to pop the tins in the oven.

Looking at me over his shoulder, Beck asks, "Why's that?"

"Because I think your bread is better. And I like watching you." A month ago, I would never have thought to share my thoughts so brazenly, but seeing the joy Beck gets from my unfiltered honesty only spurs me on.

"You really like my bread?" Beck asks, stalking toward me with a small smirk tugging at the corner of his mouth.

I tilt my head back to meet his gaze, my mouth also quirking up. "Would I lie to you?"

"No, you wouldn't," Beck answers as he cups my face with my one hand, his thumb brushing lightly over my cheek.

It gives me great satisfaction that he knows that I wouldn't. Having his trust means so much to me.

Beck smiles down at me, his tone completely sincere as he says, "I can't give you a list of everything I like about you, because I don't think we'd have enough time. It's practically endless."

"Aren't you the charmer?" I tease, leaning into his hand.

Beck tilts his head to the side. "Is that a good thing?"

I nod and place my hands on his hips, relishing how good it feels to touch him so freely. "For me, yes."

"Then, I'll try to charm you some more. But first, do you want to play some chess while we wait for dinner?" Beck asks, the offer of a familiar game a welcome suggestion to break all the sexual tension brewing between us.

"I'd love to. I might be a bit rusty, but I think I can still beat you." Maybe a little friendly competition would help me think with my head and not my pussy. Surely chess can't turn sexy.

"You can try," Beck says, his tone holding a challenge as he heads over to the gaming cupboard. "Our last match didn't end well for you."

I cross my arms over my chess, pretending to sulk. "We were twelve. I dare say I've gotten better over the years."

"So have I." Beck gives me a cocky look as he sits down opposite me and starts arranging the pieces on the board.

My breath hitches at the confidence in his tone, sending a bolt of lust straight to my pussy. It feels like Beck's implying he's good at other things too. Judging by the way he's kissed me, I'd wager to say that's very true.

Feeling bold, I throw down my own challenge, "What should we make the winner's reward?"

Beck shrugs. "Anything they want."

I think on that for a second, then suggest, "How about the winner picks where they sleep tonight?"

Looking up, Beck pauses with the white queen in his hand, his brows drawn together. "What do you mean? Where else would you want to sleep?"

I reach forward and lay a comforting hand on Beck's forearm, not wanting him to think I have plans to be anywhere else but here with him. "I mean, the winner can choose to sleep on the couch or the bed tonight."

Eyes flitting between mine, I see a thousand thoughts pass through Beck's head before he finally settles on a neutral response. "I guess that's fair."

Beck finishes up setting up the game for us and soon we're lost in strategies, trying to predict the other's next move, all while our legs remain intertwined under the table.

Beck lays a hand on my thigh, not in an overtly sexual way, but his soft caresses have me squirming in my seat. My mind strays from the game and to other fantasies about what those hands can do, my pussy getting wetter with each minute that passes.

Feeling like two can play at this game, I clear my throat and reach up to get the pins holding my slicked-back bun together. Beck's mouth gapes open as he watches me undo my hair, and I may put on a little show of shaking it out, letting the long locks fall down my back.

"That's unfair," Beck almost pants, his hand tightening on my thigh as his eyes roam over me.

"What's unfair?" I ask, playing innocent as I card my fingers through my hair, hoping they don't snag on a knot and make me lose the sexy vibe I'm trying to exude.

Beck pauses mid move, scales fluttering all over his body. "You know how much I like your hair. I'm going to keep staring at it and then I can't focus on the game."

"That sounds like a terrible problem to have," I joke with a fake pout.

Thankfully Beck picks up on my tone, because the next moment he lurches forward and wraps his hand around my hair, tilting my head back and stealing my breath with a voracious kiss.

There's nothing tentative about this kiss, no teasing in the way Beck's mouth dominates mine, only pure passion as the rest of the world fades away and I surrender to my best friend.

I gasp as Beck scoops me up with one arm and positions me on the table, chess pieces clattering to the floor, our game now blissfully forgotten. Beck presses against me and my legs wrap around his waist as he kisses me like a creature who's been starved for too long. I meet every stroke of his tongue with one of mine, eagerly returning every bit of fervent emotion he's pouring into me, telling Beck with my body that I feel it as much as he does.

Beck's hands dip below my blouse and we part only long enough for him to strip it off me before our mouths meet again, devouring each other with even more urgency. My hands move hurriedly to the buttons of his shirt, my fingers fumbling to undo them as Beck presses wet kisses along my jaw and down my neck.

My pussy is soaked, and I'm on the verge of undoing his pants, ready to beg him for his cock—or cocks—right here in the kitchen, but then Beck pauses to sniff the air and groans, his forehead flopping against my shoulder.

For a split second I feel self-conscious enough that maybe he's scenting me, but I quickly shove those intrusive thoughts far away, because surely he'd be happy to know how much he's turning me on and won't be disgusted by how I smell. Or maybe—

Riiiiing.

The oven timer goes off and Beck lets out another forlorn groan as his arms tighten around my waist. "That's really unfortunate timing."

"You knew it was going to go off?" I ask, still breathless where I sit in only my flimsy camisole, trailing my fingers through Beck's silky strands.

Beck nods against my shoulder. "I could smell the bread is done, so I knew it was going to go off soon."

"Oh." Am I disappointed that we had to stop right when things were getting good? If I'm being honest with myself, yes. But maybe it's for a good reason. We're meant to take things slow, and whatever was happening here just now, was anything but slow.

It was hot. To the nth degree hot.

"I'm so sorry to interrupt... this," Beck says, finally making eye contact with me, my heart melting at the true disappointment in his blue gaze. "I need to take the loaves out of the oven or else they'll burn and no one will get bread tomorrow, and I won't have dinner for you either."

"For us," I correct, stroking a lock of fallen hair off Beck's forehead.

"Us," Beck repeats softly, placing the lightest of kisses against my lips before settling me back on my chair and heading over to the oven to take out the freshly baked spinach-artichoke stuffed rolls.

I knew I was attracted to Beck, knew I liked him for his sweet heart and quirky personality, but seeing this new side of him is going to take me a minute to process. And a lot of self-control to withstand tonight, or however long until the time is right.

No matter what, I have to end up on the couch tonight or we'll just be repeating all of this again, or more.

BECK

CHAPTER 15

After dinner, Eleanor helps me clean up and I relish in the domesticity of it all. She belongs here, with me, in this home. I don't know how I'll ever convince her of that, or when I'd even have the courage to suggest it, but I know I want a life just like this, with Eleanor. I feel like I can really make her happy, hopefully as happy as she makes me.

Putting the last plate away, Eleanor leans back against the counter, the moonlight shining down on the dark ocean behind her framing her like the prettiest of pictures. "We didn't finish the game, but we both know I was going to win," she teases.

A slow smile creeps across my mouth. "I had a strategy. I was enjoying watching you back yourself into a corner."

Eleanor narrows her eyes at me playfully. "Sure you were. We'll just need to have a rematch another time. But all this to say that as the projected winner, I get to choose where to sleep tonight, and I've decided I'll take the couch."

"No, you won't," I state, refusing to accept that as an option. "You take the bed. I'll stay down here."

Eleanor crosses her arms over her perfect, full breasts, and my mind strays directly to all kinds of filthy thoughts about what they'll look like if I happen to take off that silky camisole of hers, wondering what they'll feel like in my hands, imagining myself playing with them, sucking on them, and—

"That's definitely not happening," Eleanor says, effectively cutting off that train of thought. "You're too tall and won't fit. I'll take the couch."

I shake my head, not seeing the need to even have this conversation. "Over my dead body. You've had a bad day. I'm not letting you sleep on that uncomfortable thing."

Eleanor chews on her lip for a second, then she meets my eyes, a pretty pink spreading across her cheeks. "We can share the bed?" she suggests shyly.

"That makes a lot more sense. Come." I take Eleanor's hand and lead her up toward the mezzanine level, then point at my bed. "This is the bed. I like to sleep on the right, but I can switch if you prefer that side."

"The left is good with me. I get to see the sunrise first then," Eleanor says, taking a look around the sparsely decorated room, pausing to lift onto her toes and staring out the eastern window facing the darkened island.

Too late, I realize I don't have any curtains up here. I've never had anyone in this bedroom before, never mind having them stay over, so the thought has never crossed my mind. What if Eleanor feels uncomfortable? Should I hang a sheet to create some kind of covering?

I try to see my bedroom through Eleanor's eyes, hoping I don't disappoint her too much. My bed has a simple navy duvet with gray pillows placed against a headboard made from reclaimed wood. The brown from the stone walls and the brown of the floorboards might be too masculine for her taste, but if Eleanor ever decides to stay with me, I'd be happy to change things—everything, if she wants.

On the windowsill, I've placed a couple of plants, one being lavender that I requested from Annamae recently, and the others a mix of herbs I use for baking. Maybe it's odd that they're in my bedroom, but I like their smell and I didn't think much of it before now.

Nerves climb up my throat, threatening to take my ability to speak, my hands getting clammy as I wait for Eleanor to say something.

Rescuing me in the nick of time, Eleanor squeezes my hand. "It's really cozy up here, calm. Thank you for letting me stay."

I breathe out a huge sigh of relief and cup her face with my free hand, "Anytime."

We stay frozen like that for a long moment, letting my offer settle before I ask, "Can I give you something to change into?"

Eleanor laughs. "Have you seen my boobs or my butt? There's no way your clothes will fit me, but thank you for the thought."

That surely can't be a serious question, could it? Of course I've seen her beautifully curvaceous figure. I fantasize about it almost every night.

Before I have enough time to form an adequate response, Eleanor tucks her hair behind her ear, her gaze somewhere around her feet, as she asks, "Is it okay if I sleep in my camisole and underwear? It's only that I don't think I should sleep in my work clothes because I'd have nothing to wear tomorrow if they get all wrinkled. I just... I really don't want to make you uncomfortable. You don't have to look, maybe close your eyes while I quickly get under the covers?"

"Why wouldn't I want to look?" Letting my eyes leisurely travel over every single one of her lush curves, I answer honestly, "I can say I've noticed everything about you. You're absolutely delightful to look at."

Eleanor's scent blossoms and I breathe it in deeply, enjoying the effect my words have on her. This evening was the first time I was able to properly scent her arousal, and traces of it have surely embedded themselves into my home. The fact that I'll get to be reminded of what transpired on my kitchen table, even when she's not here, makes the thought of the looming week without her a little more bearable.

Though, I'd have to air the house out tomorrow before the guys get here. I don't particularly like the thought of them knowing what she smells like, even less if they were to bring it up in conversation.

Wait, is this what Bodin feels like when I comment on Tilly's scent? I will need to watch what I say to him in the future.

"You really want to look?" Eleanor asks, shifting her wide-eyed gaze to me.

"Should I say no? Would that make you feel better?" I ask, not sure what to do right now.

Eleanor looks up at me and takes my hands in hers. "Beck, you've just made my day. Well, you made my day by showing up in Cape Easton in less time than I thought possible, and then you made it by kissing me until I forgot that I'm supposed to be scared of the ocean, and then... Well, this is the cherry on top."

I move Eleanor's hands to my waist and glide my fingers up her bare arms until I cup her face between both of my hands. "Would you like it if I told you more often how pretty you are? How beautiful you look when you wear those dresses with the tiny straps? How dirty my thoughts get when I imagine what you'd look like without any of it on?"

Eleanor's heart races faster and faster, her pupils dilating and her breathing shallow. "Yeah? I wouldn't mind hearing more of those thoughts."

I trace her bottom lip with my thumb. "Okay. Get in bed and I'll tell you more."

Leaning forward, Eleanor takes my thumb into her mouth and sucks lightly on it before she backs out of my embrace. My heart stutters and my jaw drops at the move. I want her to do that again, but this time on my cocks, but I quickly remind myself that tonight isn't about me or my wants.

Holding my gaze, Eleanor unbuttons her black slacks and slowly strips them off, laying them neatly over the back of the chair.

My dragon hums in approval, just as excited to have Eleanor here, and sends as a cascade of scales down my torso and toward my cocks. The scales don't fade away this time. I can feel their hardness rubbing against my clothes, but there's no discomfort, no need to fight my dragon on this.

I'll take good care of her, I promise him. Satisfied with my answer, he makes himself scarce, disappearing within my chest as my eyes graze down Eleanor's gorgeous thick thighs, my hard cocks stiffening even further.

"Fuck, you're a dream," I breathe out, unsure if the words are audible to Eleanor.

She unclips her bra under her white camisole and in some strange move, pulls it off without removing the upper layer. Eleanor groans with relief the second her bra is off, her breasts now free and finally taking their natural form.

This image of Eleanor has me salivating, and I reach down to adjust my cocks, not wanting any more attention on them. This is all about Eleanor. The woman who looks like she's stepped out of a classical painting by a very gifted artist, only to grace me with her presence.

Tonight, my only focus is her. I want to give Eleanor a reason to be happy she came here, a reason to come back often. I want to enjoy every tiny detail, cement it in my mind so I can remember it forever.

I remain still as Eleanor slowly pads toward the bed. When she notices the weight of my gaze, it's as if confidence is poured down her spine, her steps getting surer as she saunters the final distance. It makes me so proud of her, because Eleanor has absolutely nothing to be shy about.

"Your turn," Eleanor says, her eyes devouring me as I reach for the buttons of my shirt.

I take my time, meticulously unbuttoning my shirt, reveling in Eleanor's attention and feeling like I'm soaring above the ocean with the power of her attraction for me. I turn my back on her only long enough to hide my cocks as I pull on my loose sleeping pants, then I flick off the mill's main light, plunging my home into darkness except for the lamp on Eleanor's side of the bed.

Letting the peaceful sound of the waves lapping at the shore wash over me, I welcome the familiar creaks of the mill's gears, the occasional groans of the ceiling's wooden beams to soothe any nerves that might stand in my way to make Eleanor feel truly appreciated.

I still can't believe my luck that I have my childhood best friend here, in my bedroom, when I once thought I'd never see her again. I'm not about to let fate down for giving us a second chance.

Stopping at the foot of the bed, I grin down at the most gorgeous woman I've ever seen. "Lie down, my lovely Eleanor. Let me tell you the story of your beauty."

Eleanor sucks in a shaky breath, but she does what I ask, scooting down from her spot against the headboard until she's lying flat on her back.

I get in next to her and prop myself up on one elbow. "Is it okay if I touch you a little while I tell you which parts I like the most?"

Licking her lips, Eleanor nods slowly while she looks at me. "Yes, please."

"Since you ask so nicely, I'll start with one of my favorites." I brush my fingers through her fiery locks, letting the strands sift between my fingers. "This hair. This crown of flames only fit for a queen. It's your most striking feature and, like a moth to a flame, it never fails to draw me in."

Eyes softening, Eleanor leans into my hand. "Thank you, but you're actually the one with the pretty hair."

I press my thumb against her lips, effectively silencing her. "This is story time, Eleanor, and you're my muse. I intend to give you a very happy ending before you're allowed to change books."

My muse's lips tip up into a pleased smile, halting any further arguments.

Slowly, I work my way down, tracing my fingers over each of Eleanor's features as I tell her about them. Her warm honey-brown eyes, the elegant bridge of her nose, her pouty lips and the way they curl up at the corners when she's even just a little happy, the softness of the skin below her ears and the sweet sounds she makes when I kiss her there, and finally I pause on the light dusting of freckles across her shoulders, which remind me of my favorite constellation of stars.

"Can I keep going?" I ask, my voice gravelly with desire.

"There's more?" Eleanor's chest heaves, her perfuming arousal filling my olfactory receptors, telling me she likes this as much as I do.

My smirk comes easily. "This story is far from done."

I drag a finger down Eleanor's sternum, watching her face for any hints that this isn't something she wants. She nods at me, and with a slight arch, pushes into my hand as I move to cup one breast over the silk fabric.

The rough groan that escapes me is part dragon, precum leaking from my cocks as she fills my hand abundantly. "Do you have any idea how beautiful you are? These breasts were designed by the gods themselves, making mere mortals weep at not being bestowed the honor of being blessed with them."

Eleanor's mouth parts and I can see she wants to say something, but she decides to stay silent, her scent getting stronger and her heart racing underneath my touch.

I glide a finger toward her nipple, drawing concentric circles around the bud until a stiff peak forms underneath her camisole. "I've had dreams about these. Wondering what they'll look like, wondering what it'll take to get them hard, wondering what they'll taste like in my mouth."

Eleanor almost hyperventilates as I give her other breast the same attention, her eyes flicking between my face and my fingers.

My hands skims down her stomach, and she sucks in her belly, the action making me pause. "Why did you do that?"

"It's embarrassing," Eleanor mumbles, not quite meeting my eyes.

I turn her face back toward me. "I can't see anything that could possibly be embarrassing about any part of you. There's not one thing I'd ever imagine changing. To me, you are perfect."

"Fuck," Eleanor says, her hands reaching for me. "*You're* the perfect one."

I raise my brows. "Did you get your happy ending yet?"

"No?"

"Can I continue with my story?"

Eleanor lowers her hands again, answering sheepishly, "Please."

Slowly, my hand drifts over her hip and I cup her ass, relishing how good it feels to knead her flesh. "This ass, Eleanor. This is... I don't know if I have adequate words left to explain it."

"You don't need any more words, Beck. Please just don't stop touching me."

Something about the way my name sounds makes me hesitate. It doesn't feel right, not with Eleanor when we're together like this. Not when this means so much more to me, when Eleanor means so much more to me. I want her to call me by my real name, the way she used to do.

Letting my vulnerability show, I ask quietly, "Can you call me Shinsu? Please?"

Eleanor lifts a hand to cup my face, something like adoration shining in her eyes as her thumb brushes across my cheek. "My sweet Shinsu, of course. And can you call me Nori again?"

I fold my fingers around hers. "Nori," I breathe out, her name a prayer across my lips. "My beautiful Nori. That feels so good to say again."

Something settles between us, like the right key slotting into a lock after searching for it all your life.

I swallow hard as my eyes stay locked on Nori's, a deep understanding passing between us as I skim my hand down her thigh. Nori licks her lips and parts her legs, inviting me for more.

Ever so slowly, I move higher, until my fingers touch the seam of her underwear. Scales appear on my arms and along my torso, but for not a single second do I allow them to distract me from the beautiful woman in front of me.

Nori and I breathe in unison, every breath shallow, our hearts beating as one, as I glide two fingers over her soaked panties.

"Shinsu, please," Nori begs, one hand on my cheek, the other on my chest, looking just as desperate as I feel.

"I'll never deny you." I kiss her palm and dip my hand underneath the fabric.

Keeping my eyes locked with Nori's, I glide my fingers lower, finding her wet and needy.

Nori gasps, her eyes rolling back in her head as I slowly sink two fingers into her drenched core. Getting to see her like this is a gift I don't take lightly. Earlier in the kitchen, things might have moved fast, but this here is an experience I want to cherish.

"Show me what you like," I say as I lean down, rubbing my nose along hers, my voice holding a pleading quality I hardly recognize.

Nori arches into me and her hand grabs the back of my neck, holding me to her as sweet little whimpers fall from her lips, her enjoyment of my touch sending ripples of satisfaction down my spine.

"Shinsu, yes," Nori moans as my thumb finds her clit, her grip on me tightening.

The way my name sounds when she says it makes pride I've never felt for the weighty title flood my veins, and a desire to reclaim its meaning and make it my own burrows into my heart.

I lean back only far enough for our eyes to meet and hold, reading every minute cue, monitoring her scent, her heart, her breathing, and her face as I draw tight circles around the swollen nub until Nori is clawing at me, her hips rolling, asking me for more.

"That's it. That's my girl," I praise, feeling like a king that I get to be the one who gives Nori pleasure.

It's the most intimate experience of my life, being this connected to Nori, having her allow me such unguarded access to every single one of her emotions as her cunt starts to tighten around my fingers.

I increase the pressure on her clit, pumping my fingers faster in and out of her, pushing against the sensitive spot inside of her, building her toward her peak.

"Yes, just like that. Don't stop, Shinsu," Nori gasps as she rides my hand, her lids lowering as her legs start to tremble.

Then, I watch in awe as she falls silent, her pleasure cresting, her cunt pulsing around my fingers as I guide her through her orgasm until she falls back, limp and sated.

When Nori's eyes open again, I make sure she watches me as I pull my fingers free, bringing them to my mouth and sucking them clean. I hum with satisfaction, pleased to finally know she tastes just as good as she smells.

Feeling utterly gleeful, I pull Nori into my arms and get ready to sleep.

"I didn't even get to touch you," Nori says drowsily.

"Tonight was all about you," I remind her. I don't think Nori knows about dragon anatomy, but tonight certainly wasn't the right time for that conversation.

"Tomorrow. Tomorrow, it's your turn," Nori mumbles.

I'm not sure if there will be time tomorrow, considering our busy schedules, but there's no rush from my side. I plan to have Nori in my life forever, and this is only the start.

ELEANOR

CHAPTER 16

Before I even open my eyes, a wonderfully blissful smile stretches across my face. I turn over and reach for Shinsu, ready to cuddle and maybe even start the day off by returning last night's favor, only to find his spot empty and cold to the touch. My eyes fly open as my hand connects with a note, and I quickly scan over Shinsu's neat handwriting.

Good morning, my muse
I ran out for a couple of errands early this morning, but I hope to be back before you even open your beautiful eyes.

If I'm delayed for some reason, please feel free to use the shower, or stay in bed as long as you'd like. Do anything you want.

My home is your home.

-Your Shinsu

I press the letter to my heart as I gaze around Shinsu's bedroom, then indulge myself with the urge to squeal and kick my feet out of pure giddiness.

My Shinsu. That's who he is, who he was, and who will always be. It's like I'm living the dream my young self secretly wished for, but this is so much better. And Shinsu is so much hotter than I could've predicted. Nicer too. And sexier. And that voice of his... yum.

I reread the note again, allowing an unrestrained smile to spread across my face. Perhaps past me would've taken the sentence about the shower as Shinsu telling me I stink, but based on how many times he sniffed me last night and all the comments he's made about my scent, I know that's not the case. Part of me almost considers not even washing. However, it's book club day and there's no way I'd do that to any of the other creatures with sensitive noses.

I wonder if they'd be able to tell something more has happened. Lucille totally would if I showed up in my work clothes as opposed to my usual Starry Hill-only dresses. Would anyone ask me about it? Would they be curious?

Who am I kidding? There aren't any real secrets in this small town. All the Starry Hill creatures know everything about each other.

The thought motivates me to get out of bed and I quickly tidy the room before I head over to the bathroom to clean up. I debate with myself whether I should wash my hair or not, counting the days since my last everything shower versus the risk of walking around with untamed curls without my straightener here. Perhaps it wouldn't be as noticeable if I put my wet hair in a bun after?

Decision made once I spot Shinsu's range of products, I grab the lavender shampoo and pat myself on the back for stepping out of my comfort zone yet again. If this keeps going I might even consider myself adventurous soon.

With freshly washed hair still dripping down my back, I stand in my towel and stare down at my work bra, mentally cursing the underwire that's going to be stabbing me all day once I wrestle my breasts into the torture device.

"Nori?" Shinsu calls, and I automatically check that all my bits are covered even though he's literally had his hands all over me, and *in* me, last night.

A thrill races down my spine and goose bumps tingle along my skin as I replay some of Shinsu's words followed by that look of complete devotion while he made me come.

"I'm in here," I splutter, trying to clear my mind so I don't stink up the place again, then open the door a crack.

Shinsu stops outside the bathroom and his eyes take a moment to scan every visible inch of me before he breathes out, "Good morning."

I bite my lip and my cheeks burn as I grin back at him, opening the door further so he can see all of me. "Hi." In the back of my mind a sliver of insecurity niggles at me, wondering if Shinsu thinks I look like a drowned rat, but I squish that unwelcome thought like the pest it is as a flurry of scales erupts along Shinsu's arms and he reaches down to adjust himself.

A couple of seconds pass where Shinsu simply stares at me as if he doesn't believe I'm really here, then he holds out a paper bag. "I brought you something to wear," he says after clearing his throat. "And a toothbrush. And a hairbrush. And lotion. I don't know if this is all you need, but we can get more stuff from The Winged Apple later."

Taking the bag from him, I glance at the contents, my heart inexplicably full at the thought and effort he put into this. Yesterday, Shinsu asked me to trust him. He told me we'd figure something out. And he totally delivered.

Never before have I felt so taken care of as I do with Shinsu, and I can only hope he feels the same from me too. No matter what, I'll do everything in my power to protect him and make things work between us. I want Shinsu to be my happy ending.

I put the bag down and move forward to fling my arms around his waist. "Thank you. Thank you so much. For everything."

Shinsu holds me to him. "It's my pleasure. I'd do anything for you."

Looking up at him, I whisper back, "And I for you."

I duck away before Shinsu can lean down to kiss me, needing to at least brush my teeth first. "Sorry. Let me get dressed quickly and get rid of this morning breath, then I'm all yours."

"Is that a promise?" Shinsu asks, propping one arm against the doorjamb.

"If you want it to be."

At this point, I'm going to stop overanalyzing everything I say. So what if things are moving faster than a conventional relationship? It's been months since Shinsu and I reconnected and we communicate more openly than I do with anyone else. We're both consenting adults—enthusiastically so—and we both want to be together.

For so much of my life I've been timid, but I'm done holding back and filtering myself. With Shinsu, I feel safe to speak my mind and share my true feelings. And I hope he feels the same about me too.

I lather myself with lotion and brush my teeth before I tackle my hair. Squeezing some conditioner into my hand, I start crunching my hair while I think back to my brief rebellious phase in university when I wore my hair curly. I knew nothing about proper curly hair products, still don't, but normal conditioner helped define my curls and reduced the frizz enough to look somewhat presentable. That phase only lasted long enough until my mother called me to berate me after seeing a picture online, reminding me of the professional image I need to exude as a lawyer.

But this is now and I refuse to live in the shadow of the past. I like the idea of looking authentically me. And it would save a lot of time and energy if I stop restricting myself and conforming to other people's standards, especially the ridiculous ones my mother set for me.

If no one else is freaked out by how weird I look without my sleek strands then I might delve into proper curly hair research when I get home. But before I invest in a whole bunch of products, I'll let today be a little test run.

With my copper ringlets looking somewhat presentable, I take out the lilac dress from the bag. The moment I hold it up, a note falls to the ground and I quickly pick it up.

Eleanor,

This is my lucky dress. It's basically responsible for Bodin falling in love with me. Remind me to tell you the story later!

May you have just as much luck as I did! Though, based on Beck's face this morning when he came by, I don't think you need any ;)

Can't wait to see how pretty you look at book club later!

Love, Tilly

P.S. It has a very supportive built-in bra, so no need to stress about the proper undergarments.

Practically buzzing with excitement, I place the note on the counter. I love letters and getting two before I've even had breakfast, has my heart feeling full and so, so grateful for the people in my life. When I get to The Dancing Daisy later I'm going to get myself a scrapbook to save them. Plus, I'm going to ask Shinsu to write down the amazingly romantic things he said last night and maybe it can turn into a little book of affirmations for me.

Holding Tilly's dress up, I silently thank her for lending it to me, hoping that her luck is still attached to it too, before slipping it over my head. I relish in the comfortable fit of the built-in support and I stick my tongue out at my inessential bra and the monochrome outfit I don't have to don on such a happy day.

"Something smells amazing," I say as I enter the kitchen, the aroma of freshly brewed coffee filling the air.

Shinsu's thrown open all the windows, allowing a gentle breeze to pass through the old mill as the waves lap lazily at the shore. It's the most idyllic picture with Shinsu leaning against the counter, the early morning sun sparkling on his scales as he studies me from across the room.

"Please pause right there," Shinsu says, his hands flexing on the counter behind him.

"Okay?"

Shinsu's eyes flit all over me, first fast, then he drags his gaze up in a slow caress—up from my bare feet, up over the dress, lingering on my generous cleavage, before taking his time going over my lips, eyes, and down again, following my hair. "I want to memorize you like this. The way the ringlets frame your face, the way the strands twist and curl—you're ethereal, Nori. Breathtakingly beautiful. But mostly, there's something new about your expression today I want to remember. It's the way you look at peace with the world and yourself."

Tears fill my eyes and I whisper back, "It's because I am. I'm exactly where I'm meant to be. Just as I am."

Shinsu meets me halfway and then I'm in his arms, our mouths colliding, wordlessly expressing the feelings we're not able to verbalize yet.

During breakfast, Shinsu explains that he stopped by Bodin and Tilly's cottage first, knowing they're always up before dawn, and asked Tilly if she had something that I could borrow. He knows I carry an extra pair of flat shoes in my bag for all the walking we do in Starry Hill, so that wasn't a worry for him to procure.

He also braved waking grumpy Pierre from sleep in order to get some supplies from The Winged Apple. When the old gargoyle heard it was for me, he insisted on getting the best quality of items and instructed Shinsu to return with me later to create a list of necessities for future stays. The thought of spending whole weekends with Shinsu in Starry Hill already has me deliriously delighted.

One item we didn't think of, though, is underwear. No way am I putting on my soaked panties from last night. I'll just have to go without, and hope no errant gusts of wind come my way. Or fingers. Though, maybe on my way home I wouldn't mind if Shinsu went exploring and his fingers happened to find my aching pussy before we have to say goodbye again for a week.

But for now, I'm locking away all dirty thoughts and turning my attention to book club and enjoying every single second of my day with Shinsu and my friends.

Beck

Chapter 17

Everything looks bright and new this morning. Birds chirp gleefully in verdant trees and a tranquil breeze whispers through the tall grasses as Nori and I walk hand in hand along the cobbled path toward The Dancing Daisy.

In my chest, my dragon is stretched out on his back, lazing peacefully as he basks in the feeling of having Nori by our side. It feels great not to be at odds with him lately, our hearts united in prioritizing Nori. Neither of us even pushed to go for a swim this morning, not while there were so many other things we could do to bring a smile to Nori's face the first time she stayed over.

Being with Nori like this feels so natural, so perfect, that I can't imagine my future without her in it. I'm already dreading having to say goodbye again later. If I had it my way, she'd quit that job that makes her so unhappy, move in with me, and lie on the couch all day, reading to her heart's content. I can take care of her. I want to take care of her. We could—

Interrupting my daydream, Nori asks, "Does Lucille know about us?"

My brow pulls down as I consider that, wondering if I messed up. "Yes. Is that okay?" Wanting to be as truthful with her as possible, I add, "I asked her to help me with ideas to court you, and she suggested the candies since you've been wanting to try them. I also saw her early this morning for our weekly tea date, though I only dropped off her bread and couldn't stay for actual tea. But I did promise to have a cup during book club. Besides, she shooed me away very quickly when she heard you stayed with me, and said she didn't want me to leave you alone too long."

A smile lifts the corners of Nori's mouth. "That's really kind of her. I'll be sure to thank her later. I'm sorry that I kept you away though."

I shake my head. "I'm not. And don't worry, we've decided to move our Saturday tea dates to Monday mornings." Lucille and I discussed the possibility of Nori staying over more frequently and that it might interfere with our usual schedule, so moving the date to a weekday made the most sense. I'd hate being distracted while spending time with Lucille, which is a big possibility if I knew Nori was waiting for me in my bed.

Nori stops walking as concern bleeds into her voice. "I hope it's not because of me."

My dragon sits up and pushes against my chest, wanting to reassure Nori. Reading my intention, he relaxes again as I brush my thumb across the back of Nori's hand. "Of course it is because of you. But in the best way possible. Lucille likes that I have a... special someone. And she's happy that someone is you. It was her suggestion to change the days."

"I also like having a special someone," Nori says, her gaze bouncing between my eyes and my mouth.

Unable to resist, I band an arm around Nori and draw her against me. She lifts onto her toes as I lower my head, our lips meeting in the most gentle caress. We remain like that for a while, simply breathing each other in, before I reluctantly loosen my hold on her and we continue toward the island's biggest hill.

After a short while of walking in companionable silence, Nori squeezes my hand. "Can I ask you a big favor?" The question is slow, her voice unsure, coming out like she's doubted if she should even ask it.

"Of course," I say easily, not seeing one thing I'd ever deny her.

Nori can't quite meet my eyes as she asks, "Can you maybe write down some of the nice things you said last night? I'm going to need them to sustain me during the week until I get to see you again."

My feet slow to a stop and I turn to Nori, tipping her chin up to meet her sparkling eyes. "Of course. I can come up with even more, because my muse never ceases to inspire me."

Pulling her lip into her mouth, Nori tries to hide her pleased smile. "Really?"

I take a quick look around to make sure we're still alone while my dragon scents the air. He gives me a nod of approval and sends scales flitting over my cheeks and down my jaw, relishing in the way Nori's eyes track the peacocking move.

"I can write chapters dedicated to your scent," I whisper against her neck, dipping low to nibble at the base of her throat. "Especially the way you smell right here."

Nori tilts her head to the side, granting me more access. "Uhm, maybe you shouldn't do that."

I lift my head to meet her eyes again, confused at the different signals I'm getting. "I'm sorry. Did I do something wrong?"

"Not at all," Nori says quickly. "It's just... I'm not wearing any underwear, and if you keep touching me or kissing me, all of Starry Hill will probably smell it."

"What happened to your panties?"

Pink steals across Nori's cheeks. "They kind of got a little wet last night. Can't really wear them again."

Skimming my hands down her sides, I let my palms rest on her hips, feeling no evidence of underwear under my fingertips. "So right now you only have this dress on. Nothing else?" I ask, my voice gruff with lust, barely resisting the desire to bunch her dress up and see for myself.

"Yup." Nori pops the *p* as she traces the scales on my chest. There's a teasing glint in her eye, almost like she knows the effect she has on me and is enjoying it very much.

Needing her to fully understand how much I want her, how much I desire to please her, to worship her, I cup her ass and pull her against me. "Nori, if book club wasn't one of the most important things in your life today, I'd be throwing you over my shoulder and carrying you home so I can lick your cunt over and over again until you come on my face. Then I'll—"

"No. Don't tell me," Nori pleads with a laugh, pressing a finger to my mouth. "If you keep going I'm going to be dripping down my legs before we get there."

I open my mouth enough to swirl my tongue around the tip of her finger, a tease of what I want to do. "I can always lick you clean."

"Shinsu," Nori gasps, her scent blooming beautifully.

Kind of seeing her point, and not wanting to share that part of her with the rest of the town, I relent. Partially. "Okay. After book club, and then all night long."

"What about your game night with the boys?"

Oh fuck. I totally forgot about them. Should I cancel Knights and Castles tonight or would that be too rude considering we canceled last weekend too? I'm not ready to say goodbye to Nori so soon. But how to balance it all?

"I can take you home after?" I suggest slowly. "Or you can stay another night? They won't mind if you hang out with us. You can sit on the couch and read while we play."

"I'd like that," Nori says with a coy smile. "But only if you're sure."

"With you, always," I reply. In the back of my mind I wonder how I'm going to concentrate on books this morning and a campaign later when I have so much to look forward to with Nori after.

My dragon spins in circles a couple of times, elated at how well everything is going with Nori and excited about the prospects of our future. Together.

I help Nori set up for book club, carrying a couple of chairs over from The Singing Seahorse next door, but when I try to arrange them in a neat row facing the pair of orange chairs, she quickly takes over and rearranges them in a loose circle.

"I really appreciate your help, but I think maybe this way it looks more collaborative instead of like a lecture," Nori says with a slight wince as she places her hand on my forearm.

"That makes sense." I look around the room, shifting my weight from foot to foot, wondering what else I can do to distract myself so I don't pull Nori into my arms and kiss those beautiful lips the way they deserve to be kissed.

Like Lucille can sense I need direction, she glances at me from the refreshments table where she's laying out napkins. "Beck dear, would you mind restocking the candies while Eleanor and I finish setting up?"

"Of course." I lean down and limit myself to giving Nori a quick kiss, lingering only long enough to enjoy the way she sways into me before I disappear into the back room and go about my routine of refilling all the jars for the display wall.

I'm on the second jar when my dragon lifts his head, sensing someone new arriving. Halting my movements, I strain my ears and recognize Maisie's cheerful humming. My dragon relaxes again but remains wary, knowing there will be many creatures around Nori today. It's not that we distrust anyone in particular, but she's our priority and keeping her safe and happy is of paramount importance to us.

Maisie gasps loudly as she enters The Dancing Daisy. "Fucking hells, Eleanor! You look magnificent. I love your curls! Is this your natural texture?"

Nori's response is very demure. "Thank you. It's definitely something to get used to, but I'm kind of enjoying how it feels."

"That's the most important thing," Maisie says wisely. "As long as you're comfortable in your body then it's no one else's business. Though, I hope Beck has been showering you with much-deserved compliments. You really do look beautiful."

I want to shout, "Of course I am because my Nori looks like the epitome of feminine grace today." Instead, I stay quiet and let the women continue their conversation.

A bashful huff of a laugh escapes from Nori. "He has been quite generous with his kind words."

Hearing Nori say that makes me think back to last night and how much she enjoyed me telling her exactly what I think of every lovely feature of hers. Not only will I write down some of the things I've already told her, but from today I'll be keeping a notebook that I can fill with letters and thoughts I have of her each day.

I honestly think I won't ever run out of complimentary things I can say about my Nori. Beyond thoughts pertaining to her beauty, there's much to say about her sweet heart, her smart brain, and her quick wit too.

"I'm glad," Maisie says. "If he doesn't treat you right then you just let me know. I'll gather the girls and we'll go have a talk with him."

Thankfully, Nori is quick with her refusal. "There won't be any need for that."

"Good. Want to see your book club's first themed cupcakes?" Maisie asks, seemingly ready for a change of topic.

There's a sharp intake of breath from Nori, then she exclaims, "Maisie! These are gorgeous!"

Peeking out from the back room, I quickly glance at the quaint cupcakes and the bloody knives sticking out of them, glad that Maisie truly matched the theme of the book, before I resume my task.

"Thank you. I'm really proud of how they turned out," Maisie says. "Very on theme for our murder mystery, don't you think? And the knives are edible. And of course it's just raspberry compote and not blood and guts bubbling out of the frosting."

"You're a genius," Nori praises. "And thank you for coming. I'm so happy to have you here."

"I wouldn't have missed it for the world. Seriously," Maisie emphasizes. "Sorry I didn't RSVP earlier, I just wasn't sure if I could stay for book club because I had an order for a birthday cake that also had to be delivered this morning. Thankfully Ren offered to take it into Cape Easton for me so I can be free to attend. You can imagine the list of instructions I gave him to deliver that cake in perfect condition. Thank fuck he has a tail to use for extra balance. Well, that tail is good for many other things too, if you know what I mean. And Viggo volunteered to take Ren and the cake so Beck could be here for you."

"What?" Nori breathes out. "I didn't know." Satisfaction rolls through me that I was able to organize everything to be here for Nori today. Eliciting Viggo's help wasn't that hard to do once I explained to him why I couldn't ferry creatures to and from Cape Easton today. Turns out that Starry Hill really supports courtship.

Maisie continues, "It's really all good. Ren's happy to help. He's sad he had to miss book club though, because we read the book together. Maybe he can join for the next one."

Lucille joins the conversation as they discuss other book and cake pairings, and slowly more creatures filter into the shop, each one making some kind of favorable remark when they notice Nori's lovely curls. I move at a snail's pace in the back, wanting Nori to live in the moment without me stealing any of her attention. She deserves all their accolades for what she accomplished today.

Starry Hill truly values community, and Nori has created a new opportunity with this book club for us bibliophiles to come together. But the cherry on top of this literary cake is how much Lucille loves the fresh light Nori has been able to shine on The Dancing Daisy and the way she's breathed new life into the shop.

I recognize Peregrine's voice as the satyr asks someone, "Can you believe Beck missed karaoke last night? He's never missed a night that I can remember." The owner of Starry Hill's clothing store, The Crowned Boot, has always enjoyed a good gossip session, and I guess it's my turn to be the subject of their discussion.

Unsure if they know I'm here in the back, I keep absolutely still as I process this observation. I do enjoy karaoke, but I always sing the same song. It didn't even enter my mind to go last night once Nori was in my arms. Perhaps we can go together next weekend and we can duet the song. That's a suggestion I'll be sure to make later.

Marisol speaks next, her yawn still apparent as she says, "Can you blame him? If I had Eleanor with me, I wouldn't want to go anywhere." I didn't think the siren would come today, considering how late she usually closes the pub on weekends. It makes me so happy to know that the town is showing up for Nori, even if it's not strictly convenient for them to do so on a Saturday morning.

Maisie's voice is filled with innuendo. "Eleanor, hope you made it worth his time and serenaded him with your own voice all night long. Or did Beck give you a private performance?"

I can just imagine Nori's blush as she replies neutrally, "I haven't heard him sing in years. But we used to make up dances and sing together all the time as kids."

Peregrine hums conspiratorially. "Well, every Friday night is karaoke night. You have to come next week and join us. It's so much fun."

Not even daring to breathe, I wait for Nori's response. "I'd love to, but I don't know if my schedule would allow it. I often work late, so it might be tight coming here straight after work and making it before everything's over."

"Just move here already. We know you want to," Maisie says, sounding very eager to have Nori a permanent part of the Starry Hill community.

My dragon bolts upright, pressing his head against my chest to hear Nori's answer as nervous scales flit over my skin. Sharing my anxious thoughts with my dragon, I bombard him with a flurry of questions. *Will she refuse? Will she say she's considering it? Shouldn't I be the one asking her these questions? What do we do if she says yes? What do we do if she says no?*

Lucille's voice pulls me back from my panic spiral as she tells the others, "Stop harassing Eleanor. Let her take her time."

Nori's tiny sigh is barely audible, so I quickly shuffle some boxes, making a little more noise so human ears can pick up on my presence before I exit the back room with the refilled jars and stack them in their proper locations.

Tilly waves at me from across the room. "Morning, Beck. You staying for book club?"

"Of course," I answer simply and incline my head at the other creatures in attendance, a few more than RSVP'd. "Shall I get more chairs?" I ask Nori, quickly counting heads and finding we're now at eight attendees instead of the five we expected. Nine, if I count Aurelius, the mothman who owns The Lonely Rake next door, hovering by the entrance.

"Yes, please. I think we need a couple more, if you don't mind," Nori says, placing a hand on my arm. Everyone else fades away as I look at the most beautiful woman in existence and I fight against the urge to pick her up and carry her home so I can make love to her until our bodies are spent and our souls are aligned.

Tilly's voice cuts through my notions. "Both Doc Calla and I wanted to come today, but one of us had to man The Bandaged Heart. We had to flip a coin to help us decide who got to come, and the other will join for next month's pick."

Richard, who brought themed pies from The Flowering Teapot, had a similar experience with Annamae, but she graciously let him come today while she stayed behind to tend to their customers.

Peregrine simply decided to close his shop, saying the first new event on the calendar is more important than the few stragglers who'll come peruse his clothing store on a Saturday morning.

Eventually, everyone is seated after a few of us carry more chairs over. They snack on cupcakes and pies while sharing their thoughts on the book, discussing plot points and favorite characters. A few came with notebooks, others with annotated copies so similar to how Nori writes in the margins of her own books.

I enjoy every second of watching Nori in her element, talking about all the Easter eggs and red herrings and how they're woven into the romance subplot, even if it's still a mystery book.

Maisie sits forward in her seat and everyone's heads turn to look at her. "I totally liked the mystery of it all. And the fact that he killed the competition so he can be sure to get the girl. I mean, is there anything more romantic than a guy stepping out of his comfort zone to win your heart?"

That thought has my attention. Have I stepped enough out of my comfort zone for Nori? Can I do more to win her heart? I know she's said she's mine, but how do I fully convince her to move in and spend the rest of her life with me?

There are a couple of noises of agreement from the others before Maisie continues, "My only complaint is where was the smut? The ravishing? I wanted him to rip her clothes off. No, for her to rip his off when she realized what he's done and reward him for all his effort."

Ravishing? Ripping clothes off? *That,* I can do. I've wanted to do that and explore the curves hiding underneath Nori's clothes for months. Last night I had the privilege of getting a small taste of her, but I'm ready for the full meal, to devour Nori and...

"Yeah, I agree," Aurelius says with an enthusiastic nod, bringing me back to the present. "This book would've been perfect if there was a deliciously smutty reward for the reader at the end." Throughout the meeting, Aurelius positioned his seat closest to the door so he could hear if a customer needed help at his shop, popping back to assist them before returning to the discussion.

Peregrine wiggles his eyebrows. "Or in the middle." The smile the satyr sends the mothman's way has Aurelius's feathery antennae twitching excitedly.

Tapping her pencil against her notebook, Nori asks, "So you're saying you want more smut?"

Maisie balls her hands and brings them to her chest. "We *need* smut. All the smut."

"Scandalize us," Marisol adds, waving a hand against her face like she's hot.

Would Nori want to be scandalized? Would two cocks be considered scandalous for a human?

Tilly holds up a finger. "But still give us plot."

Peregrine adds, "And a mystery."

A slow smile creeps over Nori's face and she leans back in her seat. "Mission accepted," she purrs.

In this moment, Nori looks so comfortable and so sure of herself while being the center of everyone's attention. The sight of her at ease like this, talking about a topic she's truly passionate about, makes pride bubble up in me, scales slowly flowing over my chest as my dragon echoes my thoughts.

I knew I loved Nori, but realizing just how much almost brings tears to my eyes. It takes monumental effort not to be swept away by my emotions and to sit still while she continues to shine in what looks to be her natural habitat.

"It's not too tall of an order?" Lucille asks Nori with a tilt of her head.

"I might have just the book for that," Nori says and starts ticking off on her fingers. "It has a little bit of mystery and a whole lot of smut. It has an FMC escaping a sex cult, and a knight ready to annihilate anyone who dares harm her, but he keeps telling himself that he doesn't have any real feelings for her."

"Yesss," Maisie practically growls. "Give me more of that. I love some secret pining. Where do we sign up?"

Nori looks around the room and studies the different expressions of everyone present. "Would you be interested in different types of book clubs? Like one can be more smutty romance and one can remain as closed-door mysteries where romance is only a subplot? You don't have to answer right now, I'll have a signup sheet on the refreshment table after this, but if you're comfortable with it, maybe by a show of hands, how many of you would want to join for the smutty romance pick?"

Almost everyone raises a hand, and I quickly raise one in support too. If Nori is coming to Starry Hill, then I'm doing everything and anything to spend more time with her. I've never read a smutty book before, but from what the other women have been hinting at, I might just learn something from them.

Richard clears his throat. "I'll raise a hand for Annamae. And one for Calla. They already read a lot of romance, so having others besides them and Lucille to discuss their type of books with might be fun. And if that book comes in audiobook format, even better. Annamae likes to listen while she bakes. But I'll keep to the tame mysteries, if that's okay."

Aurelius hesitates for a couple of seconds before he finally asks, "Is it possible to meet on a Sunday afternoon or evening? That way more of us can attend and don't have to worry about our own shops or have to close them."

"That's very thoughtful of you, Aurelius," Peregrine says, effectively causing the mothman's entire face to turn pink, his wings giving a small flutter of pleasure at the compliment.

"Yes. Then we can alternate meetings. One week mysteries, one week smutty picks, and we can add more if you're up for it," Tilly suggests as she absentmindedly rubs her stomach. "But don't feel pressured to say yes to any or all of it."

There are more murmurs of agreement, and Nori steals a quick glance at me. Her voice turns shy as she says, "I can ask Beck if he wouldn't mind ferrying me about so much."

It feels weird to hear her call me Beck again, but I'm glad she did so in front of the book club, because I'm only Nori's Shinsu. For now. When the time is right, I'll reclaim the name fully. But not before I explain to Nori why I stopped using it in the first place.

"He doesn't," they all answer in unison.

I echo, "I don't." And silently add, "This way I'm sure to have you all weekend, every weekend."

Maybe it's too soon to ask Nori if she wants to move in with me, even if she'll only stay on weekends, but just in case she says yes, I'll clear out half of my closet and prepare her a reading corner this week. I'll do anything to turn my old mill into a place that she can call home, somewhere she'll always feel welcome and loved.

ELEANOR

Chapter 18

This lilac dress must be lucky, because today is one of the best days of my life. Not only did book club go seamlessly, but the community wants more. My brain is already spinning with ideas for different book picks and themed events, perhaps even craft days too.

The prospect of coming out here every Friday night after work—schedule and workload willing—and staying all the way until Sunday evening, perhaps even Monday morning, it has me feeling all sorts of giddy. Who knew my life could be this good? That I could be this happy?

A tiny part of me, hidden all the way in the back of my logical brain, is telling me that this can't last forever, that something is going to go wrong, but I refuse to accept that. Right now, I'm going to stay present in this particularly delightful day and blissfully bask in what I consider to be my nirvana.

From my position on the couch, I steal yet another glance at Shinsu, taking in the concentrating furrow of his brow as he leads Bodin, Ren, and Arran on their Knights and Castles campaign across the realm to slay the monsters and rescue the princess. I've been pretending to read all evening, but I've secretly been listening in on them, enjoying the way Shinsu narrates and the clever way his brain works with this world he's designed and the challenges his knights have to overcome.

It's fun seeing this part of him, of witnessing him in his creative element, especially after everything that transpired between us last night. He can be so literal at times that I didn't know he had such a gift with words. Watching him hold the guys captive with the way he weaves the narrative, and considering how I felt when my body became the object of his inspiration—his *muse*—I wonder if Shinsu has ever considered writing his own book. It's something I want to suggest to him later.

Shinsu glances up at me and catches me looking at him. His light eyes drag over my face, going lower until they rest on my breasts. The intensity in his gaze makes my heart race, my pussy giving a quick pulse at remembering his earlier promises for what to expect once the guys are gone.

I quickly cross my legs in case I start broadcasting the direction of my thoughts to his friends too, just as Arran finishes telling the guys about something his knight is doing.

The longer the game continues, the more distracted Shinsu gets. A couple of times, the guys have to repeat what they said, subtly redirecting Shinsu's focus to them when he goes silent while his attention is on me.

My book is simply a prop to hide behind at this point as our stolen glances turn into heated stares, my body growing hotter with each lengthened perusal Shinsu gives me from across the room.

Closing my eyes, memories of last night flood my mind, and I mentally trace my body as I try to recall each comment, each compliment, as Shinsu showered me with praise. I think about the sensation of his hand, the whisper of his words, the feeling of surrender as Shinsu guided me over the edge and I truly realized I was in love with him.

My eyes flow open at the thought of telling him that, only to find Shinsu already watching me.

Our gazes meet.

They hold.

Shinsu's jaw ticks as the moment stretches, his chest rising and falling faster and faster.

My heart speeds up too and my breathing grows shallow as Shinsu's eyes darken, his scales becoming more pronounced on his arms and his neck.

Ren pushes his chair back. "Thank you for a fun evening, but we've got to go. We'll pick this up again next Saturday."

Bodin looks at Ren, then at Shinsu, and also stands up. "Thank you for a delicious meal. Good to see you again, Eleanor."

Arran takes a minute to catch up, then finally pushes his chair back too. "Oh, I see. Have a good evening."

Shinsu doesn't say anything as they leave. He remains seated as more scales appear, his gaze still firmly locked on mine as the guys' voices grow fainter outside.

Every second that passes, my pussy gets wetter, my nipples hard as they push against the fabric of the dress. My whole body is strung tight, anticipation coiled as I wait for Shinsu to set me free.

"Nori," Shinsu nearly growls, his chest heaving as he takes a long sniff. "Is your cunt feeling needy?"

"Yes," I whisper back, my pussy feeling unbearably empty.

"What do you need, my muse?"

"You."

In a flash, Shinsu is up and rushing across the room, his mouth crashing against mine as he pulls me into his arms. He lifts me up by the back of my thighs, wraps my legs around his waist, and then he's carrying me up the stairs, his steps hasty but sure as I kiss, lick, and nibble on every inch of skin I can reach.

Shinsu lays me down on the bed, his mouth trailing down my throat and over my chest before he pulls my dress down, freeing my breasts. "Look at these gorgeous tits," he says, lowering his head and sucking a nipple into his mouth.

I gasp at the sensation, my back arching. "That feels so good, Shinsu."

"I love the way my name sounds when you say it," he rasps, moving up to kiss me again while his hands knead my breasts.

"Shinsu. My Shinsu," I repeat against his lips as my hands pull him to me, needing him closer.

His voice is pure gravel. "Fuck, yes. Tell me exactly what you want, Nori. Tell me where you need me."

I don't have to think about my answer. No doubt exists in my mind that Shinsu Beck is what I want most in this world, to be with him, to love him, to make a life together.

Taking his face between my hands, I whisper, "Make love to me, Shinsu. Make me yours."

"Fuck," Shinsu breathes out shakily. "I've been waiting for you for so long. If I make love to you now, there's no going back. Losing you again will destroy me, Nori."

My smile is small but sure. "You're not losing me again. I'm here. I love you. I want you. Forever."

Shinsu's eyes widen and he lowers his forehead against mine. "I love you too. So much. You consume my thoughts every second of every day." He lifts up only far enough to read my expression. "But I don't deserve you. I still need to explain what happened all those years ago and why I left like that. I need your forgiveness before I can truly receive your love."

Pressing a finger against his lips, I say, "You can tell me later. I've already forgiven you. I trust you, Shinsu."

"Fuck, Nori. That means so much to me. I promise to make it up to you. But first, let me show you how much I love you."

Together, we stand up and slowly undress each other. Our moves are meticulous, thoughtful, and reverent as our hands map every dip, every curve, taking care with each piece of clothing.

I undo the buttons of Shinsu's shirt, one at a time, as our gazes stay locked. With each new inch of skin revealed, I press kisses against the exposed flesh, over scales rippling under my touch, taking my time to appreciate Shinsu's beauty.

Adoration is in Shinsu's touch as his mouth moves over my shoulders, my breasts, down my stomach, before my dress lands in a pool on the floor and I'm completely naked before him.

"You're so beautiful, Nori. I don't think I really knew desire until you came into my life again." The complete devotion in Shinsu's eyes as he stares at me makes me feel like the most important person in the world, confidence flooding my veins, every last hint of self-consciousness drowned out while I remain the object of his desire.

Slowly, I reach for the button on Shinsu's waistband. He takes shallow breaths as his eyes stay focused on mine and his pants rustle to the floor.

I reach down to cup him, but when I don't make contact with a cock—or two—Shinsu wraps his hand around my wrist, effectively halting my movement.

"Do you know about dragon anatomy, my sweet Nori?" Shinsu asks, rubbing a thumb across the inside of my wrist.

"I tried to read up on it," I admit. "But there's not much information online."

A small smirk pulls on one side of Shinsu's mouth. "We're very secretive creatures since there aren't many of us. I'll tell you everything you want to know about us soon, but first, let me show you what dragon cocks look like." Smirk fading a little,

Shinsu adds, "Please don't be alarmed. You don't have to do anything you're not completely comfortable with."

Tracing the scales over his heart with my free hand, I promise, "I love you just the way you are. A cock, or cocks, don't change anything."

"Okay."

The tips of my fingers graze against a slit, and my brows pull together as I try to make sense of what I'm feeling. Looking down, a thin snakelike tail protrudes from the slit and wraps around my finger.

Oh. This is... unexpected.

Does Shinsu not have a cock? Was that some false rumor online? I'll love him regardless. This is just going to take a minute to process.

Before I have the opportunity to reassure him, a second tail joins the first and I suck in a breath as this one also curls around my finger.

This was probably what the articles said about two. Maybe they can stimulate my clit? I'd be open to experimenting.

Placing a knuckle under my chin, Shinsu tilts my face up. "These are my cock whiskers. They resemble my dragon's sensory whiskers that we use to gauge irregularities in the water, helping us sense any threats. They're prehensile and can add extra stimulation where you most desire."

"Kind of like antennae? Are they sensitive?" I ask, rubbing my thumb over them.

A shudder rolls down Shinsu's body, scales trailing in their wake before congregating around his slit. "Very," he answers huskily.

I'm already thinking about what I can do that'll make him shudder even more, but then Shinsu holds my hand still. Slowly, a much larger shape fills my palm, my jaw dropping as it grows longer and Shinsu guides my fingers across the smooth scales covering the lower half. I try my best to keep my eyes on Shinsu's, but when he moves my hand lower, and a second cock joins the first, I can't help the way my gaze drops to see what he's been hiding.

"So, does this count as two cocks or four?" I ask, letting my fingers explore the textures, slowly rubbing up and down each length.

"Two cocks," Shinsu pants. "And two cock whiskers. But don't feel like you need to take all, or any."

"I don't know if I can take both tonight, but..." Feeling shy, my voice trails off.

"But?" Shinsu prompts gently.

Knowing we promised each other complete honesty, I share the secret activity I've been exploring at home. "I may have read somewhere that dragons have two cocks, so I bought some toys to practice with. You're bigger than my toys, but I know I can take you. All of you."

"You did? You can? You want?" Shinsu stumbles through the words, a smile flickering across his face.

"Yes," I say, moving around him, enjoying how confident I feel right now. "Now sit down and let me make you feel good. Tonight you're my muse."

"Fuck, Nori. I love you," Shinsu whispers with utter awe as he lowers himself onto the bed.

Kneeling between his legs, I let my hands drift up his thighs, watching the scales trailing my touch. I wrap my hand around Shinsu's lower cock, monitoring his expressions as I apply some pressure. The moment his jaw lowers with pleasure, I lean forward and suck his other cock into my mouth.

Both of Shinsu's hands fly into my hair, gently holding my curls back as he watches me, looking astonished at how much I'm enjoying giving him pleasure. I don't want to think of others who came before me, but something tells me that Shinsu hasn't experienced much of this. One thing I do know is that from now on, he'll always benefit from having my complete devotion.

My pussy is wet, dripping down my inner thighs as I alternate between his two cocks. I let his whiskers wrap around my index fingers and suck them into my mouth too, relishing in the way the breath stutters out of Shinsu.

When I notice the way Shinsu's stomach tenses, he pulls me lightly off him. "Nori, please let me fuck you. You smell so good and I'm not going to last much longer. I need to be inside you. I'm on birth control and tested. I can show you my—"

"Yes. Fuck me, please." The request isn't even fully out of my mouth before Shinsu picks me up and lightly tosses me onto the bed.

Lowering himself between my spread legs, Shinsu kisses me like his breath depends on it while gliding his cocks through my arousal. A whimper crawls up my throat as his whiskers circle my clit and my back bows, wordlessly begging for more.

Shinsu holds my gaze as he reaches down and notches a cock against my opening, and I tilt my hips up to meet him. I have longed for him for so many years, the thought of our bodies now finally connecting the way our hearts have, has me thanking fate for allowing us to cross paths again.

The air is heavy, time stops, our breaths mingle as Shinsu slowly pushes forward, my life feeling like it's hovering on the precipice of something big. There's no going back to a time without Shinsu, no going forward without him. He is my destiny.

Shinsu fills me inch by delicious inch, while his other cock glides forward against my clit. My breath shudders at the sensation of his smooth scales rubbing against two of my most sensitive spots, but we never break eye contact. I want to witness every single second of Shinsu's beautiful face as he claims me for the first time.

When he's fully seated, Shinsu lets out a deep grunt of satisfaction and presses his lips to my forehead. "You feel so good, my muse. Pure perfection. I thought I could write you poems before, but you deserve entire novels."

Even though my heart feels full, my pussy feels needier right now. I squirm against him. "That's very romantic. But can you do that later? I need you to move. Please."

A self-assured chuckle rolls out of him. "Hold on."

Shinsu pulls back before he slams into me again, one cock in my pussy, the other caressing my clit. My fingers claw at his back, glad for his scales so I don't leave any marks as he thrusts into me over and over again.

My moans build, becoming louder and louder with each powerful drive of his hips, but when his whiskers join his cock inside me and push against my front wall, it's game over. I cry out at the new sensation, the pleasure so much stronger than anything I've ever felt before.

My orgasm crashes through me in a wave of ecstasy, reverberating from the base of my spine down to the tips of my spasming toes. Shinsu keeps going, guiding me through it, praising me, telling me how beautiful I am and how much he loves me.

I brush some loose strands out of Shinsu's face as he rolls his hips in slow, deep strokes, letting me come back to myself while his body teases of more to come.

"Wow," I breathe. "I know I loved you before, but wow." I was not adequately prepared for how good two cocks would feel. But adding those cock whiskers is a whole game changer. I'm just glad I never have to settle for anything less again. Shinsu is mine. Forever.

"You're okay? It's not too much?" Shinsu asks.

"Never."

"Think you can give me one more?"

"Come with me this time," I say, and push against his shoulder.

Realizing what I'm trying to do, Shinsu rolls onto his back and I brace my hands on his chest as I start riding him in earnest. I find a rhythm that soon has him panting, then I spit in my hand, giving his other cock just as much love the one inside of me is getting. Shinsu plays with my breasts, tweaks my nipples until I cry out, my pussy squeezing around his cock.

Sensing I'm close, Shinsu holds onto my hips as he drives up into me, harder and faster, bouncing me on his cock.

My pleasure builds into a giant peak, then I'm free-falling over the edge, my screams ringing through the night as Shinsu slams into me until he finds his own release with a roar of triumph, filling me, marking me, claiming me.

Completely spent, I collapse onto Shinsu's chest as we ride out the aftershocks of our pleasure.

"I love you, Shinsu Beck."

"I love you, Nori Landry."

Maybe part of me should care about the sticky release against our stomachs, or have questions about the cock still filling my pussy that hasn't gone soft yet, but I don't have space for one worry in my head. Right now, I'm basking in the happiness of being in Shinsu's arms, of being his, of being truly loved, and knowing this is the start of my happily ever after.

CHAPTER 19

L ife is fantastic and wonderful and exciting. All because of Nori. My beautiful, perfect Nori.

Until now I thought I understood what love was, but never did I imagine how all-encompassing it would feel to be *in* love. Every waking hour I think of Nori, in my sleep I dream of her. Each moment she's not with me I long to be together again, to wrap her in my arms, to kiss her smiles, to lay her in my bed and make love to her all day and all night.

Never have I felt this happy before.

My blood simmers with my desire for Nori and my need to claim her the dragon way becomes stronger each day. How soon is too soon to ask her to marry me? I might need to ask Bodin how long he waited to ask Tilly. Or maybe Arran can advise me on proper courtship-to-marriage protocol.

Excited about my future, I tell my dragon, *Let's go for a swim. I want to play in the water.*

My dragon perks up, his tail swinging from side to side as we head out just after dawn. He's been sulking a little after we had to say goodbye to Nori on Sunday night, but he knows she'll be back on Friday again. It's been hard to leave the house this week because we both want to be around her lingering scent, but I still have duties to fulfill for Starry Hill.

I check my phone one more time to make sure there aren't any new notifications from Nori, then head toward the dock.

So far I've filled up pages and pages in my notebook, sending snippets of my inspired thoughts to my muse as messages, and reading passages to her each night when she calls me from her place.

Some of the most fun we've had is me listening to Nori touch herself while I read to her, and her telling me how she'd satisfy me if we were together. After we both find our release, we count down the days until we can see each other again, then we exchange "I love yous" and fall asleep blissfully.

On the dock, I strip off my clothes and admire the scales that have been ever present since Saturday. Maybe they would've bothered me before, but Nori seems to like them well enough, so now I've simply accepted them as part of who I am.

I take a deep breath and shift midair as I dive into the crystalline water.

Staying under far longer than usual, I propel my serpentine body forward as the ocean washes over my heated skin. From above, sunlight dapples down onto the sandy floor and fish scatter away from me as I enter their underwater world. Ahead of me is nothing but boundless space, the ocean inviting me to explore and be refreshed as she embraces me like an old friend.

My dragon and I luxuriate in the freedom of the open water, diving down deep before bursting into the air again. Over and over again, we go under then break the surface with our horns, enjoying the way our long body feels as it undulates through the rhythmic waves.

Here, all my worries melt away and I simply exist. This is such a liberating feeling I want to share with Nori. Especially this week considering how stressed she's been with her job, much more than usual it seems. I only hope that one day she'll feel comfortable enough to join me out in the open water like this. I'll take such good care of her, teach her about the ocean, and prove to her there's nothing to fear.

Properly sated, physically tired yet feeling invigorated, I shift into my human form and set off for the town while my dragon drifts off to sleep.

All week I've been working on Nori's reading corner next to the window in the living room. I've gotten her a plush chair and book cart and other items recommended by Lucille. Now I only need to pick up the handmade blanket from Peregrine at The Crowned Boot before it'll all be ready.

I can't wait to surprise Nori tonight. I hope she likes it.

"Morning," a deep voice greets, jolting me out of my daydream.

I take a step back as I spot Arran leaning against a tree. I must be so lost in thought, I didn't sense the vampire. Not even my dragon bats an eye at him as he rolls over and goes back to sleep.

"You're out during the day," I observe.

"Aye," Arran answers. "I'm wearing sunscreen."

"I'm sure you are, or else you'd be burning," I say, walking closer. I can count on one hand the times I've seen Arran out before sunset, so this seems like more than a spontaneous walk around the island.

"True," Arran replies with a small nod. "So where are you off to on such a fine morning?"

My chest puffs out as I say proudly, "I'm picking up something for Nori. I made her a reading corner."

"Courting going well then, I assume." Arran smiles one of his rare smiles, and I wonder what it would take for him to fully feel joy the way I do today.

Would falling in love with someone unlock that part of him? What kind of creature could make him want to venture beyond the walls of his castle that he hides behind?

Putting away those questions for the time being, I answer, "Courting has been very successful. Do you think it's too soon to ask Nori to marry me?" That's the real truth I need to know today.

"Aye." The word is short, definitive, and doesn't invite further argument.

My shoulders slump as my dragon lifts his head and narrows his eyes at Arran. "But I want to."

Raising his brows, Arran asks, "Does she want to marry you?"

I sag onto a large rock as I give that some thought. "I think so. Maybe. She says she loves me. And she wants us to be together. Though maybe it would be simpler if she actually lived in Starry Hill."

Arran looks around as if he's searching for someone else to jump in and take over the conversation. I understand that he might not have a lot of experience—or any for all I know—when it comes to love and marriage, but maybe he can give me advice based on his observations of others across the four hundred years he's been alive?

Clearing his throat, Arran perches on a rock opposite me and says slowly, "That's a step in the right direction at least. Maybe take things slow. Humans can be... unpredictable."

"Not my Nori." Scales wrap around my limbs as my dragon curls back his upper lip, ready to defend Nori from such slander.

Arran holds up both hands. "I don't mean any offense. What do I know, after all? I've not courted someone in centuries. Times may have changed since I was young."

Slowly, my scales recede but my dragon keeps a watchful eye. "I'll keep that in mind. Maybe I should talk to Bodin or Tilly to get their opinions."

"They'll certainly be more knowledgeable than me regarding matters of the heart," Arran agrees.

Needing to get back to neutral ground, I ask, "Where are you going?"

Arran runs a hand over his cropped hair. "Meeting with Calla at her place. There's word of a werewolf who might need help and somewhere safe to rest for a while. We're low on space at the minute, but we'll make a plan."

"You always do," I say, noticing the dark circles under his eyes. "How can I help?"

"I'll let you know once we have a timeline on when to expect him."

"Arran?" I say after a moment's hesitation.

"Hmm?"

I take a bracing breath, then say something I should've said a long time ago. "Thank you. For back then. For finding me and giving me a safe space too."

Arran's slight smile is full of understanding. "You're welcome, Beck. That was always my intention with Starry Hill. To make it a refuge for creatures who need it most."

"I... uhm..." Staring at my feet, I admit something that few but Arran will understand, wanting to share the huge step with my friend. "I started using my real name again, with Nori."

His nod is full of approval. "I am glad to hear that."

"I hope to one day be ready for the whole town to call me Shinsu too. Not yet, but hopefully soon. First, I need to explain to Nori why I stopped using it when I moved here."

"Take your time," Arran encourages. "She seems like a good one and she'll understand. The town will understand too."

We say goodbye and continue on our separate paths. I grab lunch from The Flowering Teapot, and the softest blue-and-orange crochet blanket from Peregrine, before popping by The Dancing Daisy to show Lucille.

When I get home, I put the final touches on the reading corner and place the bouquet of flowers Annamae grew for Nori in a vase. Then, I lower myself into her cozy new chair and wait.

Things have been really busy at work for Nori this week. Regardless of working late most nights, she still makes time to talk to me for at least an hour before bed, plus she takes time to reply to love notes during the day too. I try not to overwhelm her, but for the messages to be encouraging and help her get through the day.

I know how much she's looking forward to this weekend and escaping from the city and that stupid fucking job that makes her so unhappy. I'm going to do everything in power to make her happy and forget about all her stress while she recoups here, with me and all her friends.

My first plan after I pick Nori up and feed her a delicious dinner, is to take her to The Singing Seahorse for karaoke. I'm so excited for that because we'll finally be able to perform the song we made up a dance for as kids, the same song I've been performing every Friday night for as long as I've been attending karaoke.

The sun inches closer to the horizon and I stare down at my phone just as it starts to ring. My whole body lights up as Eleanor's name appears on the screen, my dragon loping up and down my chest with equal excitement.

"Nori," I answer, a broad smile beaming from me as I say her name.

A beleaguered breath puffs across the line. "Hi, Shinsu."

Feeling like this is a repeat of an event not so long ago, I shoot up out of the chair. "Where are you? At the harbor already? Are you okay?"

"I'm still at work." Nori's voice is weak, the words sounding like she's wrestling them free.

"Okay?"

Nori hesitates then chokes out, "I... I don't think I'm going to make it tonight."

"We don't have to go to karaoke." If Nori is nervous about singing and dancing in front of the rest of the town, then I'm happy to stay home and cuddle her and kiss her and—

"I mean, I have to work late, again. I don't think I can come to Starry Hill." Nori sounds like she's holding back tears, but I can't tell if they're sad or angry.

"How late?" I ask. "I can pick you up when you're done. Even if it's the middle of the night."

"No," Nori says quickly, her voice cracking on the word. She takes a trembling breath and continues, "Go out and enjoy karaoke with your friends. Don't wait for me."

I take a couple of seconds to process what she's saying, then, needing to confirm, I ask slowly, "So, you're not coming?"

Nori sniffs. "I'm going to try my best to come tomorrow, but I can't make any promises."

"Oh. I understand." I don't know if Nori is breaking up with me, but I've had conversations like this before, and I know where they lead. My dragon's head hangs and he retreats deep within my chest as I wilt into Nori's chair. "Please take care of yourself and get some rest too. And let me know when you're ready to see me again." I try to keep my voice neutral and not to let my disappointment bleed through, even if it feels like a thousand papercuts are slicing at my heart.

"I'm sorry, Shinsu," Nori whispers.

"Me too."

"I love you."

"I love you too."

Nori doesn't come on Saturday.

She doesn't come on Sunday either.

My dragon is quiet. My scales gone. My heart empty as I remain in Nori's chair, hoping this is some kind of nightmare I can wake up from.

CHAPTER 20

Late Sunday morning, I crack my eyes open and reach for my phone, yearning for my Shinsu.

No new messages.

My heart sinks like a hefty stone. I've gotten so used to seeing his name pop up on my screen throughout the day, that the absence of it hurts more than I could've prepared myself for. Yet, I know I don't deserve to hear from him after going silent since Friday night.

Shinsu's been so good to me all week, sending me the sweetest musings and compliments, keeping my soul fed as I struggled through each day. Then at night we'd talk for hours, things getting more than a little heated before I'd fall asleep happy, knowing I'm loved, and able to brace myself for another day.

It broke my heart to cancel this weekend, but I had no choice. My boss dumped a giant project on my desk before he left for a weekend of golfing, knowing the presentation is already scheduled for Monday. Thanks to doing business with my mother over many years, he's well aware of my inability to say no and my fear of disappointing her.

Breaking the news to Shinsu was the hardest thing I've done in a long time. There was simply no way I would've been able to balance Starry Hill and my work. I was fighting back tears the entire conversation, keeping my sentences short, afraid Shinsu would detect how upset I was at the prospect of not seeing him.

Would he ever forgive me? Would he understand why I was so short on the phone?

I tried my best to get everything done so I could at least spend some time with him this weekend, but the paperwork I was given was incomplete and I needed to do more research than anticipated.

Somewhere past midnight on Friday I passed out at my desk, and once I woke I decided to remain at work until everything was entirely done. So many times throughout Saturday I picked up my phone, the desire to call Shinsu almost unbearably strong, but then I'd pinch myself before chucking my phone in my drawer again. If I heard his voice, I knew I'd cave and ask him to come save me, to take me to Starry Hill with him, and never return to this godsforsaken place.

I can't go on like this. My soul is withering away the longer I stay at this job. I hate being away from Shinsu, from Starry Hill, and my loving community there. And knowing what true happiness feels like now, it seems inconceivable to continue with life as is.

But how can I be so selfish to want a different life than the one I have right now? Shouldn't I be grateful for having a secure job, my own home, and a sweet dragon to visit on weekends? It seems conceited, wrong, to want more for myself when I already have so much.

In desperate need of advice, I stumble out of bed and throw on some comfy sweats, and head upstairs to Audrey's place.

"You look like shit," Audrey says as she opens the door.

"Thanks. I feel like it," I mumble, shuffling toward her couch and collapsing onto it.

Audrey props a hand on her hip as she studies me. "Coffee, wine, or something stronger?"

"Stronger," I groan.

"Fuck." Cocking a brow at me, Audrey asks, "That bad?"

My shoulders climb up to my ears. "Maybe?"

"On it." Audrey heads to the kitchen and comes back with a bottle of strong liquor I haven't touched since university days, and places two shot glasses on the coffee table. "Just to kick us off and loosen your tongue."

I grimace as the awful taste hits my tongue, but I swallow it down gratefully. "Gross."

Audrey pours a second shot. "Boys, work, family, or all of the above?"

"Work mostly," I cough out after swallowing down the near poison. "But I think I fucked up with my boy too."

Just the thought of Shinsu sends a pang through my heart and I check my phone again. Still no new messages.

Audrey taps her empty glass on the table. "Look, work stuff I can always help with, but when it comes to love, I'm severely lacking."

"You did pretty well last time."

Wiggling her eyebrows, Audrey asks, "That nudging go well for you?"

"Very." My cheeks burn as images of Shinsu's beautiful face flash through my head, his adoring gaze as he made love to me burned into my memory forever.

"So we're beyond nudging now?"

"We're in the 'I love you' stage now." Half of me wants to swoon at the thought, but the other half of me is too scared to allow myself to.

"Damn girl. That was fast," Audrey sputters. Hesitantly, she raises her hand. "Well done?"

I lower her hand again and shake my head. "Not well done. I haven't heard from him since Friday." Finally, I confess my biggest fear, the words quivering over my lips, "I'm scared I might lose him."

"Fuck." Audrey freezes before rallying herself again. "Usually I'm the one who dissuades women from falling in love and running after a cock or two, so I think I might need to call in some reinforcements to help us out here." Sitting forward, she takes my hand, her voice tender as she says, "I'm sure whatever happened is a simple misunderstanding and can be sorted out with a frank conversation. You're a catch and he's lucky to have you. But listen, you didn't hear this from me. Not only is Beck a hottie, he's a good guy too and I think you're well matched. If I'd wish a truly happy life for you, it would be with him. And on Starry Hill."

I squeeze her hand back. "That means a lot to me. Thank you."

"Fuck," Audrey groans, her nose wrinkled and shoulders slouched. "All the good ones are over there, aren't they?"

That pulls a smile from me for the first time today. "They certainly seem to be. Want to pack your bags and move there with me? We can live out our happily ever afters in Starry Hill." Even if I don't know where I stand with Shinsu, I'm not giving up on my dream of being together. Not until he tells me it's over.

"Yeah, that'll be the day," Audrey says with a snort. "At most I might consider a little vacation there to go help Tilly out once she pops. I might even partake in a mini fuck fest on the side. Fuck knows there might be a cock or two interesting enough to keep my attention for a little while. But only if it's no strings attached and they promise not to fall in love with me."

"You know, just by saying it you're probably going to meet someone and fall for them first."

Audrey's head rears back. "Ew. Take that talk straight to the bathroom and go flush it down the drain."

"Nah, I'm already wondering what color your cottage door will be."

Audrey rolls her eyes at me, then says, "On a serious note, I'm clearly unqualified to give you advice on your love life. Hang tight while I call a couple more knowledgeable friends."

"Thank you. Let me go freshen up a little so they're not alarmed by the state of my dark circles." Pausing halfway to the bathroom, I look back at my chaotic but bighearted friend. "You're the best. You know that?"

"Oh, talking about the best," Audrey says, already scrolling on her phone. "Don't mind the bag of dicks in the bathroom. I've been a little sexually frustrated and nothing was working last night. Cycled through a couple of options and still need to put them away after their bath."

"Thanks for the heads-up." I'm not quite sure how else to respond to that. How many dicks does one prepare oneself for? I just hope I don't see anything resembling Shinsu's cocks.

By the time there's a knock on the door, I'm a little more relaxed after being entertained by recollections of Audrey's wildest escapades. But my eyes start to water as Tilly and Maisie enter, followed by Lucille.

They each take turns hugging me, then Audrey orders enough food to feed a small army. Once everyone's settled and has a drink in hand—Tilly's being a sparkling grape juice—all eyes turn to me.

"Spill," Maisie says from her position on the floor. "We heard you had a relationship wobble and we're here to help you fix it."

"You first," I counter. "How did you get here?" Part of me hopes they say Shinsu and that he's waiting right outside the door, ready for me to run into his arms.

Tilly's smile is understanding. "Viggo."

"Not Sh— Beck?" I ask, needing to confirm. It feels weird to call him Beck, but I know how much sharing his name means to him and I want to be respectful of that. Besides, I kind of like sharing secrets with him.

Lucille reaches across the couch for me. "We haven't seen him, dear. I thought he was with you."

Tilly nods. "Yeah. Bodin thought so too at first, because no one answered when the guys went over for Knights and Castles. The mill was dark, even the gears were still."

My heart rate ratchets up as I bolt upright. "Do you think he's okay? Has anything bad happened to him?"

"He's okay," Tilly reassures me, placing a hand on my thigh. "They could detect he was at home, just not up for company."

I drop my head into my heads, a sob breaking through as I admit, "I fucked up. So much."

Scooting closer, Maisie says gently, "Tell us what happened."

Lucille rubs my back in soothing circles, her touch familiar and comforting. "Start at the beginning, dear Eleanor."

So, I do. I tell them about falling in love. How much Shinsu means to me, how much I hate my job, and how awful it is that it keeps me away from him.

"Quit," Audrey chirps, making it sound easy and like my whole life could be solved with that on word.

I frown. "Just like that?"

"Why not?" Audrey throws back at me.

Feeling like I'm missing something, I say, "I need to live. Buy food, pay rent—"

Audrey cuts me off. "Doesn't sound like you're living much right now."

The statement stuns me. A breath puffs out of me as the truth of it hits me square in the chest.

Maisie quirks her head to the side as she stares at me with compassionate sage eyes. "Why do you stay there if it makes you so unhappy? Why not find another job?"

Allowing myself to be completely vulnerable, I explain, "Honestly? My boss knows my mother. I've been a disappointment to her my whole life, with my curly hair, my bigger body, so many different things. The only thing she's been proud of was me becoming a lawyer, and after that, hearing positive things about me from my boss."

I was making so much progress on Starry Hill. There, on that tiny island with its warm community and welcoming embrace, I feel like I can truly be myself, wear clothes that make me happy, set my curls free, speak my thoughts, and laugh at whatever volume I want. But when I stepped back into my workplace, it's like my brain rewound itself, erasing my confidence, and stripping away my personality until I once again became a husk of myself—another cog in their machine.

"Toxic, gaslighting bitch," Audrey hisses.

Tilly asks, "What does your mother do to make *you* proud?"

"I..." A couple of seconds pass as I give that some thought. "Nothing."

Pulling my hand into her lap, Lucille asks gently, "My dear Eleanor, what do you really want? In your heart of hearts? What would make you truly happy? Not what's expected of you, not what you think anyone else wants you to do, but *you*, as Eleanor Landry, what do *you* truly want?"

I'm so tired of living up to my mother's expectations. I'm so tired of her voice in my head and feeling like an eternal disappointment. I want to be free. To leave behind my job, the city, and everything holding me back from living the life I want for myself.

But most of all, I want to be with Beck, to build a future with him, maybe even start our own family, in Starry Hill. Of that, I am absolutely certain. Everything else I'll figure out.

Tears well in my eyes and my voice cracks. "I want to be happy. With Beck." Pushing past the tears choking me, I keep my confession going. "I want to live in Starry Hill. I want to work at The Dancing Daisy. And eat lots of bread every day."

Lucille reaches up and wipes a tear rolling down my cheek. "I was going to discuss this with you yesterday when you came to the shop, but maybe you weren't ready for it then. Maybe fate brought us to this moment for a reason."

Around the room, everyone is silent as they wait for Lucille to continue. Tilly dabs at her eyes and Maisie gives me an encouraging smile. Even Audrey seems riveted, her glass paused halfway to her mouth.

Lucille's grin turns watery. "It's time for me to hand over The Dancing Daisy into someone else's capable hands. Someone who has loved that shop just as much as I have, someone who will continue the legacy that my Lochan's family started so many years ago."

I suck in a shaky breath, tears streaming down my face. "Lucille, that's incredibly kind of you, but I don't think I have the type of capital to buy it from you."

Shaking her head, Lucille explains, "You're not allowed to buy it. It's a gift. It's the tradition of the island, to hand over businesses when the time is right to the creature most suitable for that place."

"Lucille…"

She reaches up and wipes away another one of my tears, her own now making their way down her weathered cheeks. "I'll add that The Daisy and your relationship with Beck aren't mutually exclusive. I can say that it has helped me with the decision to know you have him on the island, a solid support system for you and The Daisy, but even if things don't work out—which we know isn't a possibility—the shop is still yours."

An ugly sob makes it way out of me and Audrey hands me a tissue, quickly dispensing some to all of us.

Lucille continues, "I love that boy almost as much as you do, but that didn't sway my opinion of you. Your dedication to the community, your love for books, your care for our Daisy, your kindness and big capacity for love, those all convinced me. So what do you say? Ready to start a new job?"

Audrey scowls at me through her own tears. "If you don't say yes right now, I'm going to punch you in the tit."

A couple of watery giggles resound around the room, then I choke out, "Of course. Yes. It would be my honor. I promise to take such good care of her."

I wrap Lucille in as tight of a hug as I dare, whispering my thanks over and over again, vowing to do my best and make our Daisy a pillar in the community.

Maisie raises a hand, her cheeks still streaked with tears. "Now that the job situation is taken care of, what's the plan with Beck?"

I look at the women as courage takes root in my heart. "Is it too soon to plan a big gesture to show Beck how much I love him? How much I want us to be together forever? Like, I want to sell my apartment and move in with him and start our lives together. Is that too weird?"

Audrey's eyes widen to a comically large degree and she visibly presses her lips together. Thankfully she knows this question wasn't directed at her and stays silent, waiting for the other ladies to give me advice.

Tilly shrugs and shakes her head. "It took me less than a week to know with Bodin."

Maisie gives her shoulders a little shimmy like she's recalling a particularly fond memory. "Ren had me from the first day I saw him. I just didn't know it yet."

Lucille bumps me with her bony elbow. "It's never too soon when you're sure. Lochan and I met, that night we made love, and we never spent a day without each other again after that."

Gaze hopping between the women, a chuckle bubbles up from me. "Holy shit. I'm slow by your standards."

Audrey takes a long swig from her glass. "The dick must be really good in Starry Hill."

Wiggling her eyebrows at Audrey, Maisie teases, "Damn straight, it is. Want to come over and find out for yourself?"

"In all seriousness though," Tilly says, nipping that line of conversation in the bud. "It's different with nonhuman guys.

Once they decide on you, that's it. Game over. Surrender your heart right then and there. Consensually, of course."

I think back to how things were when Shinsu and I were just friends, even though I had long harbored stronger feelings for him. The moment he kissed me though, I was done for and everything snowballed fairly quickly. We were on this trajectory to our happily ever after, until I had to ruin it. I only hope it's not too late to win him back.

"Okay, so big gesture," Maisie says, rubbing her hands together. "Do you have any ideas?"

My smile comes easily as I remember the bracelet sitting in my keepsake box. "I have a little something I've been saving for twenty-two years and I think it's time to show Beck how long I've kept him in my heart."

"You packing your bags too?" Audrey asks.

"I'm packing everything."

Right after I'm handing in my resignation letter tomorrow, I'm setting sail for Starry Hill, and never looking back.

BECK

CHAPTER 21

Lavender pierces my senses, but I must be mistaken. Maybe it's the plant from upstairs that I'm scenting in my melancholy haze.

Since Friday's phone call, I've not moved from this chair. I've hardly slept or eaten.

It doesn't matter. Nothing matters.

I shift into a slightly more comfortable position and pull the soft pillow more snuggly against me, a poor substitute for the feel of Nori in my arms, but it does quell the strongest ache for her.

Loneliness has always been a familiar companion, yet, it feels different now. I feel empty, a cavern now sits where my heart once was.

But I deserve this.

I abandoned Nori when we were young, and now it's only fair that she gets to abandon me. That's been the pattern of my life. The ones I love never want to keep me.

My ears ring in the quiet, and I almost imagine I hear Nori's footsteps outside, but I quickly shove that thought down.

Time has blurred together, sunlight the only markers telling me of its passage as I remain in what was supposed to be Nori's reading corner.

At some point over the past few days, I heard the guys outside and I realized it must be Saturday, but thankfully they left without any further questions. I know I have duties to return to for Starry Hill, but never has a Monday looked so bleak. I can't even muster the energy to go to Lucille's, scared of the pity she'll have in her eyes when she sees me.

A sharp gasp alerts me to someone's presence but I don't turn around to see who it is. My dragon doesn't react either, still burrowed away deep where I can't sense him.

"Shinsu," the voice says quietly as a hand lands on my shoulder. "Are you okay?"

Slowly, recognition dawns and I lift my head to see Nori's tear-filled eyes. "Nori?"

"Hi, my love," she whispers and with shaking fingers brushes hair out of my face.

I frown, not knowing if this is a hallucination or reality. "You're here?"

Nori swallows and nods with a trembling smile. "Yes. I'm so sorry for not coming earlier."

"How did you get here?" I ask, my voice hoarse after days of disuse.

"Viggo brought me," Nori says cautiously.

At this admission, my dragon peeks his jealous head out the tiniest fraction. It's a relief to know I haven't lost him forever, but I'm still nervous that this is all a dream and Nori isn't really here. I can't afford to hope.

Nori lowers onto her knees in front of me and cups my face so gently it's like a butterfly landing on skin. "Shinsu, when's the last time you've slept or eaten?"

"I don't know." My brain still feels hazy and nothing makes sense.

A lonely tear rolls down Nori's cheek. "Have you gone for a swim to settle your dragon lately?"

"No." Instinctively, I reach forward and wipe the warm tear away.

Nori folds her fingers around mine and presses my palm to her cheek. "Let's get you fed first and then in the water. I'll explain everything after."

"I'm sorry if I stink," I croak.

Huffing the tiniest laugh, Nori says, "I don't care, my love."

I swallow hard. "Are you really back? You didn't... abandon me?"

Nori's composure cracks. She shakes her head furiously, her mouth rumpling, her words an emphatic declaration. "Never. Not in this lifetime or any that follow. I love you, Shinsu. You're my forever. My happily ever after."

"Really?" I rasp, fighting back my own tears as I catch hers.

"Would I lie to you?" Nori stands and points toward the dock. "Look. My bags are outside. If it's okay with you, then I'm here to stay. For as long as you'll have me."

I take her hand in mine, halting her before she goes too far. "You brought clothes?"

"I brought everything," Nori whispers. "I quit my job too."

"You quit?" Somewhere in the back of my mind I know I should say something more eloquent, ask her better questions, but my brain is having a tough time catching up with my emotions.

Nori's smile is small as she tucks my hair behind my ear, but there's a lightness in her that has my dragon curiously creeping forward to witness everything.

"Yup. I'm not going back to Cape Easton."

True hope sparks in my chest and scales ripple under Nori's touch. "You're really, really here?"

"I am."

"Can I hug you?"

"Please."

I pull Nori into my lap and bury my face in her neck, breathing her in deeply.

Tears roll freely down my face, my back shaking with silent sobs, as I try to process everything while Nori whispers over and over again, "I love you, Shinsu. I love you."

Slowly I come back to myself, my dragon returning too, though weaker than before. "I've always loved you, Nori, and always will."

Nori presses her forehead to mine. "I'll never get tired of hearing you say that."

"I love you," I whisper again, also never tiring of saying it.

She pulls back and gives me a faux stern look. "Now, go jump in the shower quickly and then let's get you fed while I explain everything that's happened. After, we can take your dragon for a swim."

I do as Nori says, and by the time I get out of the shower, I feel a little more like myself. When I enter the kitchen, there's a bouquet of bread waiting on the table, one from each of her visits over the last couple of months surrounded by an array of spreads. My stomach grumbles at the sight of my favorite food group and my heart flutters at the thoughtfulness of the gesture.

"You prepared all of this for me?" I ask, already reaching for the cranberry orange sourdough from Nori's first visit. The aroma of the freshly baked bread fills my nostrils, my body relaxing into a seat at how familiar this feels with Nori here.

"I did," Nori says brightly from her spot against the counter. "I brought all of your favorites, but there's a new one I thought we could try. If you want?"

"Please."

Nori moves to the side and reveals a round container that reminds me of one my grandmother used to have. I sniff the air, my brain slowly placing the sweet scent. Nori bites her bottom lip as she brings it over, waiting for my reaction.

Not even looking down to check, I ask excitedly, "Is this jjinppang?"

"Yes. I've been craving them for years and finally found a bakery who has the perfect ratio of sweet red bean filling to steamed dough, just like your grandmother used to make."

Unable to resist a second longer, I lift the lid and bring the container to my nose, the aroma bringing so many memories from my childhood with it. I bite into the still-warm bread, savoring the sweet taste in my mouth before swallowing it down.

"You remember eating them with me?" I ask around my next mouthful.

Nori's mouth curls up into soft smile. "I remember everything about you. All our dances, all the snacks under that big old tree in the backyard, the chess games, waiting every year for you to arrive, and dreading the end of summer when you had to say goodbye."

Guilt rips through me at still not having told her everything. "I remember everything about us too. Can I explain why I didn't say goodbye that last time?"

Nori shakes her head, but her smile doesn't move. "Soon. First, I'm going to explain what happened this weekend while you finish eating. When you have your strength back, then you can have a turn to tell me whatever you want."

I wolf down three of the big steamed buns while Nori talks. She explains why she couldn't come, apologizes multiple times, tells me about how Lucille gifted her The Dancing Daisy, and finally how Maisie, Tilly, Lucille, and Audrey helped her pack up her belongings to move to Starry Hill to start her new life here.

Though still weak, my dragon hangs onto every word and flits scales down my skin whenever Nori needs encouragement to continue.

My heart beats faster as I realize this is really it, that there are no more goodbyes needed between us, and that fate has truly smiled down on me, letting me keep my Nori for the rest of my life.

"I have one more thing for you, my lovely Shinsu," Nori says as she reaches into her big tote bag.

Body stilling, breathing shallow, I gape at the handmade bracelet in Nori's hand. "It's just like the ones you used to make me. When did you make this one?"

Nori fastens the bracelet around my wrist, and I admire the intricate patterns as she explains, "I've been holding onto this bracelet for twenty-two years. I remember working on it for hours every night, weaving together the orange, blue, and white threads over and over again until I got it perfect. Just like I did every year for your birthday. I've always loved you, Shinsu. And a part of me never gave up hope that I would see you again."

"Wait here." With speed summoned out of pure desperation to show Nori how long I've loved her too, I rush up the stairs and dig into my nightstand drawer for the old box I've not opened in years. I race down the stairs again and place it in Nori's hands.

Slowly, Nori lifts the lid. "Shinsu," she breathes, her eyes wide as she traces the remnants of bracelets, her fingers gliding over the frayed threads of each one she made me since we were seven years old. "You kept them all?"

I pull my chair closer to Nori's and let her read the truth in my eyes. "I wore them every day until they were frayed. When they couldn't stay safely on my wrist any longer, I saved them in here, waiting for the next year you'll give me a new one again." I brush my thumb across her quivering lip. "I've always loved you too, Nori. Have you noticed the color of my front door? When I moved to Starry Hill, I was told to pick a color. Any color. I had to pick my favorite—the shade of your hair when it catches the brightest rays of the sun. Even the chairs in The Dancing Daisy I picked out for Lucille are inspired by your hair. You've always been a part of me, Nori."

Nori laces our fingers. "That last day I saw you when we were kids, do you remember it was the day before your thirteenth birthday? I was planning on giving you the bracelet the next day, and asking you to be my first kiss."

My breath is knocked out of me at the realization, and my dragon retreats guiltily into my chest. *Please don't leave*, I tell him. *That's all in the past. We're looking to the future now.*

I hold Nori's face between my palms. "Nori, I may not have been your first kiss, but I want to be your last first kiss."

"You already are," she whispers as she leans forward and presses her mouth to mine.

The world outside of us dissipates into inconsequential atoms as we breathe each other in. Our tongues caress languidly like we have all the time in the world. Because we do. Today is the start of our life together and the end of our goodbyes.

Later that afternoon, when my stomach is full and my heart light, Nori asks, "Do you want to go for a swim?"

"Yes, but let's go sit on the dock and watch the sunset together first. I want to tell you everything that happened to me the day I left."

"Okay."

Once outside, I eye the stack of luggage resting on the dock. Viggo did well with how quietly he was unloading, or maybe I was so disconnected with the world that I couldn't hear him.

I lead Nori to the edge of the dock, to the same spot we had our first kiss not so long ago, and I relish in the calm beat of her heart. She's not scared anymore and that means a lot to me.

My dragon hesitantly comes forward again and lifts his head toward the ocean, closing his eyes as he breathes in the salty air. *Soon,* I promise him. *Nori first.* He agrees wholeheartedly and gives me the space to explain our history to the woman we love.

In front of us, long, rolling ribbons of water stretch out toward the horizon and golden droplets of sunlight dance in the valleys of their swells.

I take Nori's hand in mine, keeping my gaze straight ahead as I start talking. "That day before my thirteenth birthday remains one of the happiest days of my life, because of you. But throughout that day, there was an odd sensation in my chest, almost like a scratching from the inside, and when I went back to my grandmother's that evening, everything intensified. It became an aching, roiling mess inside me, sending goose bumps all over my body which sharpened into pinpricks. My grandmother sent me to bed early with some painkillers, promising to call a doctor in the morning if I still felt unwell."

Nervous scales flicker down my arms and Nori pulls my hand into her lap, calmly tracing them as she lends me her silent support.

I clear my throat. "That night, everything got worse. The pinpricks ruptured into scales covering my entire body, and from my head... two horns sprouted. I screamed when I saw myself, effectively summoning my grandmother who screamed even more. She called my father, who surprisingly, welcomed the news. At first. There hadn't been a dragon in our line in a couple of generations, so they were unsure of what to do with me. This also meant I wasn't safe in their human neighborhood because I couldn't control my dragon. What if I shifted into his pure form right there? What if I gave away my kin's secrets? They couldn't risk it."

Memories of that night, of the fear, the uncertainty, race through my mind. I needed to be comforted, needed a friend or a parent to hold me and tell me it was going to be okay. But I got none of that.

I wasn't raised in a hugging family and physical contact was sparse, yet I still craved to be held that day, to be told I was going to be okay.

"The next day," I continue, wanting to tell Nori every single detail, no matter how hard it is to relive it all, "I was forced to stay inside while I waited for my parents to collect me. All day, I watched you from my window. The way you sat on that swing in the backyard, waiting for me to show up, it pained me more than seeing my body covered in scales. Watching you gather the courage to come knock on my grandmother's door, only to hear her tell you I went home without giving you a believable reason why, broke something in me. The image of you crying as you walked away, and not being able to do anything about it, made me vow that one day when I could control my dragon, I'd come back to you and explain everything."

"It's okay now. You found me," Nori whispers.

"I'm sorry it took so long," I whisper back. "I went to your house right after I graduated, but you were already gone." A different family had moved into Nori's at that time and didn't have any forwarding address for her. I tried to contact her mother through a number the new owners gave me, but she pretended not to know who I was. There's no need to tell Nori this right now, not when her emotions are still raw after she decided to break all contact with her mother when she moved here.

Nori shakes her head and brushes one of my tears away. "You have nothing to apologize for. My heart hurt losing my friend, but I can't imagine how hard it must've been for you to go through all of that alone."

I take in a shaky breath, knowing this story is far from done. My dragon sends scales across my chest, reinforcing me in his own way. "When my parents arrived, they were proud to announce that they enrolled me at an exclusive boarding school for magical creatures tucked away in the middle of a forest, surrounded by all kinds of wards to keep humans out. I wasn't allowed to leave there until I could shift at will and control the appearance of my scales and my horns. Some students received glamour rings to help them control their shifts, but my father refused to get me one. He said I needed to train myself and my dragon, that using a glamour ring is a sign of weakness."

Nori looks appalled at that. "Were there other dragons to help you?"

I give her a sad smile. "No. I was the only dragon enrolled at the time. I had to take many classes by myself too. It was quite isolating at times. Besides, dragons are very rare. Different families have different types of dragons connected to different elements. My family line, the Beck line, is descended from white water dragons, and our relationship is with the ocean mainly, though we can control other types of water too. In our language, Beck means white. Hence my coloring. All the males of my line have white hair and light features as a sign of our lineage, but not all get chosen by a dragon."

Nori bumps me lightly with her shoulder. "You're special."

At Nori's words, my dragon spins in a circle, optimism flowing through him and spilling into scales along my torso and legs.

"I don't always feel special," I sigh out, causing some of the scales to disappear again.

"To me, you'll always be."

"And you to me." I rest my head against Nori's while I gather my strength to finish the story, knowing she needs the whole truth if she truly wants to understand why I am this way.

"So does your father go by Beck too?" Nori gently prods.

I lift my head and stare off at the glittering golden water, letting Nori and the ocean calm me with their combined presence. "It's also his family name, but not his first name. I started going by Beck when I moved to the boarding school. I didn't want to be Shinsu there. It was too hard to remember my old life."

Tilting her head to the side, Nori asks, "So, if Beck means 'white,' does Shinsu also have a special meaning?"

I nod. "It does. 'Shin' means god. And 'Su' means water."

"So your name literally means 'god of water'? That's so fitting. I've seen the way you love the ocean, and your connection with it. To me, Shinsu seems much more suitable for you than a name related to your coloring."

My dragon agrees and gives me an "I told you so" look, undulating pearlescent scales along my limbs, much to Nori's liking as her eyes eagerly track their movement.

I give her a quick kiss then square my shoulders, bracing myself for telling Nori about the ugliest stage of my life. "After I graduated, I tried to go back home, but my parents told me they couldn't risk having me around in their human neighborhood. They bought me a boat and said it would be best to find a job where I could be useful considering my water magic and my dragon form."

Nori brings a hand up to cover her mouth. "Shinsu. That's horrible."

I swallow around the lump in my throat. "I thought I was alone before, but then I truly knew what it felt like to be completely abandoned."

"I can't fathom how hard that must've been. Did you move to Starry Hill then?"

Closing my eyes, I explain, "I spent two years working for an awful man as his personal protector. Sometimes he would ask me to shift for his delight. It made me resent my dragon for the longest time. It also didn't help that my dragon was the reason I was taken away from you and life as I knew it."

When I open my eyes again, I see Nori's are filled with angry tears, and I realize they're on my behalf. "How did you get away?"

"Arran."

"Vampire Arran?" Nori asks. "The shy recluse who's also founder of Starry Hill?"

"Yeah. He doesn't talk much about it, but he finds creatures in need around the world and offers them a safe place to live and work here in Starry Hill. He sent someone to find me too, and I packed my bags right then and there."

"That's incredible," Nori says. "I never knew that about him."

Finally, my mouth quirks into a smile as I get to a happier part again. "I've been living in Starry Hill for the last fourteen years, and my dragon and I have slowly started understanding each other and healing our relationship."

Nori reaches up and brushes some strands off my forehead. "It means so much to me that you've shared all of this with me. Thank you, Shinsu. It's a gift to know your whole past and I promise to do everything I can to keep your heart safe and make you feel as loved as you are. I'll never abandon you."

I lean into her touch. "You've helped me be proud of who I am. The way you've accepted my scales and my other dragon... attributes. Thank you. Thank you that I can be just as I am with you."

Nori climbs into my lap and straddles me, lightly tracing the scales on my chest as she looks up at me with her pure honey eyes. "You're so easy to love, Shinsu. I'm glad you've embraced who you are."

Feeling encouraged and bold, I ask, "Do you want to meet my dragon?"

Nori's head bobs up and down. "Yes, please. I've been wanting to meet him for months."

I lift her carefully off me and stand up to start undressing. Nori watches me with rapt attention, her heart racing excitedly as I unbuckle my pants. She takes over undoing my buttons, her cheeks glowing red when I stand naked in front of her.

In my chest, my dragon struts up and down, very conscious of Nori's gaze on us. He sends scales rippling over me as he gets ready to take over my body.

I press a quick kiss to Nori's lips, then I jump, shifting midair as I dive into the welcoming water.

ELEANOR

CHAPTER 22

Shinsu's dragon is beautiful. Majestic. Terrifying power coiled in a fierce serpentine body. But it's his eyes, those kind blue eyes awaiting my judgment that have me standing on the edge of the dock with an open hand outstretched toward him.

Pearly scales dance in the cascading beams of the sunset, catching hues of orange, pink, purple, and blue, painting my dragon in the most gorgeous palette. Above him, two horns, almost antlers in appearance, jut into the air, drops of crystalline water clinging to their lengths as if even the ocean is relieved to have Shinsu back in her tranquil embrace.

Cautiously, he swims back toward me, then lowers his large face until his snout bumps against my hand. Shinsu holds completely still as he patiently lets me explore him, his breathing steady but shallow so as to not overwhelm me. I love knowing him so well that even without verbal communication, I can read all his intentions.

I brush my hand along the scutes covering his snout, marveling at the tough, leathery texture, so much thicker than the scales covering his human form.

"You're so handsome," I tell Shinsu. "I love everything about you—your horns, your scales, your eyes, your teeth, the list can go on and on."

Tenderly, I lean forward and press my lips to the top of his snout, right above the sharp teeth protruding from his maw.

Shinsu closes his eyes and his mouth parts with a breath before he nuzzles into my hands. I glide my palms along all the parts of his face I can reach, tickling the soft skin under his chin, finding sensitive points, and enjoying the sight of a thrill racing down his spine.

Turning carefully as to not splash me, Shinsu shows me his back and the spiky fins racing along it.

"Like a shiver of sharks," I say excitedly. "No wonder other creatures in the ocean fear you." Shinsu frowns at that, his head lowering, but I push his chin up again so he can find my eyes. "*Other* creatures. Not me. Never me. I know I'm safe with my protective dragon."

Droplets of salty water sprinkle down on me with Shinsu's eager nodding. I giggle at the sensation and open my arms, spinning under my dragon rain, reveling in seeing this side of the person I hold most dear in the world.

"Go play with your dragon, Shinsu. Show me some of those moves you've been telling me about."

And Shinsu does. He backs up carefully before diving under, disappearing beneath the calm waters and popping up again much farther than I could've expected. He's fast. Ripples spread across the surface from his cheerful antics, sending golden sun flecks scattering in the wake of his long body undulating through the waters.

Up and down Shinsu races, going under before bursting into the air again, his joy tangible from my spot on the dock. The stark difference in mood from the creature I found this morning to who he is here, wild and free in the ocean, has me reaching for the little bows on my shoulders.

Never again will I make Shinsu doubt me, never again will he entertain thoughts of abandonment, never again will we not share in each other's joy.

My dress falls to the floor, followed by underwear, then I'm diving into the water too, thankful that my friends have arranged for privacy on this side of the island for the biggest of grand gestures.

The moment I enter the water, I can feel Shinsu's attention on me. He approaches me carefully, barely disturbing the water with his giant form, and comes to a stop in front of me, questions flitting behind his curious gaze.

Treading water, I say, "I told you I'm not afraid of the ocean anymore. Not when I have you with me."

Lips lifting into something that resembles a toothy grin, Shinsu nods.

"You looked like you were having fun. Can I play with you too?" I ask, splashing some water at him.

Shinsu's head bobs up and down again, then I'm swimming forward while he keeps a watchful eye on me. His movements remain contained as he circles me, dipping below the surface at times and appearing again at random points, carefully surprising me before dodging my poor attempts at splashing him.

Each move gets more ridiculous as he tries to make me laugh. He attempts different poses, a few quirky tricks, even blows water my way when he pops up right beside me. I belly laugh at his more ridiculous stunts, and love every moment of playing together.

Fearless with my big dragon by my side, I allow myself the freedom to explore the ocean, letting her tranquility wash over me, rejuvenate me, as the world outside of us ceases to matter and we bask in our joy.

When my limbs grow tired, Shinsu's gaze shifts into something mischievous and he stares at me from straight ahead.

A surprised shriek escapes me as bubbles tickle my feet. I kick out at them, but stop when I notice Shinsu's smirk.

"This your handiwork?" I ask breathlessly.

Shinsu's head dips with a yes, then he carefully circles me again as more effervescent bubbles climb up my legs, stopping just below the apex of my thighs. I relax into the sensations, letting Shinsu pull me toward his lowered face where he watches me with a feverish glint in his eyes.

"Oh." I register what his gaze is implying. "Yes."

A satisfied growl rumbles out of Shinsu and I bite my lip, anticipation rolling through me as the prospect of exploring something totally new between us.

My heart speeds up as the bubbles extend upward, covering my body with tiny, pleasurable tingles. More bubbles dance around my puckered nipples while others slip between legs, pulling whimpers from me with their playful teasing, priming my body for what's to come.

Parting my legs, I invite Shinsu to keep going, needing more.

Shinsu's magic keeps me afloat while he sends bubbles to strum my clit with steady pressure, knowing exactly what I like. Dipping his head down, his reptilian tongue darts out in another request.

"Yes. More," I encourage him.

A long, broad tongue unfurls from Shinsu's giant maw, and I moan wantonly as he drags it up from my belly button, between my breasts, to my collarbone.

The moment the sleek tongue passes over one of my nipples, I gasp, my back bowing at this new sensation. My hand shoots forward and wraps around one of his tendril-like whiskers extending from his snout.

Shinsu gives a low, rolling groan, almost reminiscent of a purr, then we're moving. I grab onto his other whisker and Shinsu moves faster, my head never lowering beneath the ripples as he speeds us back toward shore.

Wrapping a clawed foot around me, Shinsu lifts me onto the dock. His heated gaze takes in my naked form as I sit on the edge, and I realize what his intention is.

Scooting backward, I lower myself onto my elbows and step my legs apart so Shinsu can see the evidence of my arousal.

He breathes in deeply, his scales shimmering in the last remnants of the sun as a tremble makes its way down his long spine. Ever so slowly, Shinsu lowers his head, his eyes staying locked on mine as he inches closer.

My heartbeat has relocated to my clit, my whole body is strung tight as I pant with anticipation.

"Please, Shinsu." I don't recognize my pleading voice, but I don't care. I need more. I need this connection with him.

Shinsu opens his maw, his sharp teeth hovering above my abdomen as he drags his broad tongue through my pussy and flicks my clit. The obscene moan that is ripped from me echoes across the water, but I couldn't care less.

No longer as hesitant, Shinsu licks me again, this time with more vigor.

Underneath him, I squirm, pleasure building at the base of my spine as I noisily ride my dragon's face. But I need more. I grip onto Shinsu's whiskers and he gives a low growl again as he bucks against the dock.

Realizing these whiskers are just as sensitive as his cock whiskers, I get an idea. I bring first one, then the other to my mouth, and suck on them.

Shinsu whimpers and it's the most charming sound.

"That's it," I encourage. "Does my dragon like that?"

Shinsu's grunt of affirmation turns into another whimper. Spurred on by his reaction, I do it again. I relish in the way Shinsu shudders and groans, but not for one second does he let up on me.

His tongue plunges into me, filling me, making my back arch and my toes curl. My eyes close as I submit to Shinsu's ministrations, my whole body wholly belonging to him.

Over and over again, Shinsu fucks me with his tongue, feasting on me like I'm his new favorite meal, drawing wicked sounds of pleasure from me that I didn't even know I could make.

My orgasm barrels into me with the force of a tidal wave, bubbling through my veins, as my pussy pulses around my dragon's tongue.

When I open my eyes again, human Shinsu is hovering over me. His wet shoulder-length hair glows silver in the twilight, and from his head, two horns, so similar to his dragon's, jut upward.

Never before have I felt in so much awe of someone as I do him.

Shinsu doesn't say anything, his pulse hammering in his neck as he waits for me to speak first.

Cupping his jaw, I say, "You're incredible, you know that? Majestic. Mine."

He leans into my touch. "You're the incredible one. You let me, my dragon, do that." After a second he adds, "You don't mind the horns staying?"

"I love the horns. They're magnificent. Very elegant."

Shinsu gazes down at me with such fierce hunger it makes my pussy jolt. "Want to try holding on to them when I fuck you later?"

I let my hand glide down and find his slit, letting his cock whiskers wrap around my wrist before I fist the base of his cocks. "Fuck me like I'm yours, Shinsu. I want to take all of you tonight."

Shinsu's cocks throb under my touch. "All? Are you sure?"

"Yes."

In less than a second, I'm in Shinsu's arms and he's carrying me toward his—*our*—mill.

Beck

Chapter 23

Racing to our mill with a beautifully naked Nori in my arms, my heart hammers with the knowledge that this is it, she's mine, and tonight I get to fully claim her. Never again will we be separated.

Nori caresses my scales, placing wet open-mouthed kisses on them, stoking my need higher and higher with each loving touch.

"I can't wait to feel you inside of me," Nori whispers against my ear before sucking my lobe into her mouth. The sensation rockets through me and shoots straight down to my hard cocks.

Seeing this side of Nori, one where she can confidently state what she wants, is a revelation, and I'm already salivating for more requests from her. She's my queen and I'll do anything to satisfy her.

"Fuck, Nori. I'm going to be so good to you," I promise through ragged breaths.

"I know," my muse purrs, and sucks on my pulse at the base of my neck.

My feet almost stumble, but I catch myself quickly and speed the last few steps toward our home.

Unable to wait a second longer, I press Nori's back against the orange front door, wrapping her legs around my waist. "Do you know how long I've wanted to do this? To see your gorgeous hair matched up with the color that has haunted me my whole life? You're a dream come true."

"Being in your arms like this is my dream come true."

Not needing any more words, we dive forward at the same moment, our mouths colliding in a passionate kiss. There's nothing elegant or careful about this kiss, it's all tongue and teeth, a devouring need for each other.

My hands dig hungrily into Nori's flesh, pulling her closer, swallowing every delicious little mewl she makes.

"One day, soon," I rumble between kisses, "I'm going to fuck you right here against this door. But not today."

"Shinsu," Nori pants as her short nails scrape against the scales on my back. "Now. Please. I need you."

I nip at her bottom lip, enjoying the way her breath hitches. "If you want to take both my cocks, you have to be prepped first. I need to stretch your pretty pussy so you can fit all of me."

"Please, Shinsu. Stretch me. Take me. Fill me."

Nori's words draw a desperate groan from me, making precum drip from my cocks, my need for her at an all-time high.

"Inside. Now," I growl against her mouth.

Nori reaches behind her and opens the door, and I have just enough mindfulness to duck my head, letting my horns pass safely under the lintel before I kick the door closed behind us.

"Welcome home, my Nori." I stride straight toward Nori's reading chair in the corner and lightly toss her onto it. She takes only a second to look around and register all the book paraphernalia, her eyes widening as realization dawns.

"You made this for me?" Nori asks, her hand gliding across the soft fabric of the chair as she scans the book cart.

I kneel down on the floor in front of her. "Of course. We can change anything you don't like, but I wanted you to have something that's totally your own in our house."

Nori cradles my face and presses a soft kiss to my mouth. "It's perfect. I'm sorry I didn't realize what it was earlier, you were all I could focus on when I arrived."

"Good." I grip her hips and pull her closer toward me. "Now I want you to focus on me again while I fuck this pretty cunt with my fingers until you're dripping for my cocks."

Nori's scent blooms at my words, flowing over my senses like a pleasant balm to my soul with the knowledge that she wants all of me just as much as I want all of her.

Never did I think I could be this lucky in my life, and I almost wish I could tell my childhood self to keep dreaming because one day he'll have everything he wished for—a nice home, a view of the ocean, a community who cares about him, and the woman who's held his heart since he was seven years old.

I glide a finger up the inside of her thigh, tracking the goose bumps that follow my touch. "Do you have any idea how beautiful you are? When you're spread out underneath me like this, you look like a gift sent straight from the gods."

"Really?" Nori's question turns into a delicious moan as I slowly part her pussy lips and push a single finger into her wet heat.

"Such a tight little cunt," I croon, crooking my finger on the exact spot that has her shuddering.

Nori whimpers as I add a second finger, arching her back beautifully as she reaches for me.

Meeting Nori's eyes, I say, "Here." Then, I guide her hands to wrap around my horns. The sensation of her reverent touch on a part of my body that once scared me, is liberating.

Nori's lips part as her hands glide up and down horns and an exquisite smile graces her lips. "They're really spectacular, Shinsu. They suit you."

Finally being unburdened, finally being free to simply be me, where I get to have a future with the person I love, and her accepting and celebrating all of who I am, is the most wonderful feeling.

Inside my chest, my dragon grins at me. His happiness at us finally feeling whole is a palpable sensation fizzing through my veins. Something clicks into place between us, a new type of understanding as all our wants and needs align.

Maybe part of our contention was me fighting him when he knew what was good for me and actually wanted to lead me somewhere I could truly be happy. He saw the truth in Nori long before I even entertained ideas of courting her.

From now on, I'll welcome his guidance just as I've welcomed my scales and horns.

"You like them?" I ask. "Then, hold on tight to them while I make you come."

Slowly at first, I pump my fingers into her cunt just the way she likes. My other hand reaches up and pinches her nipples, making her cunt pulse with the sensations. I thumb her clit, building Nori to a peak, but not letting her fall over the edge. Not yet.

Nori moans beautifully as I add a third finger. "Good. So good. Keep going. I can take more."

I ignore my leaking cocks as my gaze devours the sight of Nori writhing underneath me, her pussy stretched around my fingers. Even my scales have settled as her pleasure becomes the sole objection of my attention.

"Let me hear you, Nori. Tell me how much you like my fingers," I say as I add a fourth, reveling in the way Nori grinds against my hand, begging me for more.

"I love your fingers. And your cocks. And you. Please, Shinsu. I need... I need..." Nori's pants get faster, her cheeks are flushed, her moans wild and abandoned as I finger fuck her, getting her tight pussy ready for two dragon cocks.

I lock my eyes with Nori's and lower my head, "That's it. Almost there." I replace my thumb with my tongue before sucking on her clit.

Nori detonates. She screams as her body convulses, her fingers tightening around my horns as she holds me to her and rides out her pleasure.

"That's my girl," I praise while I keep licking at her, savoring the taste of her release.

"Amazing. Best orgasm of my life," Nori says breathily as I pick up her limp body and carry her upstairs.

Laying her on our bed, I give myself a minute to simply stare down and admire her perfect body. My eyes graze adoringly over every feminine curve, from her full breasts, over her soft stomach, down to her thick thighs.

"Do you know how often I imagined you just like this? Having you naked in my bed so I can explore you with my fingers, worship you with my mouth, and fuck you with my cocks?"

Nori arches her back, confidently putting herself on display for me. "You don't have to imagine anymore."

Climbing onto the bed with one knee, I place my hand on her ankle and slowly work my way up until I'm cupping a breast. "No, I don't. You're so much better than I could have ever dreamed up."

Nori gasps and reaches for me. "You too. I love your horns, your scales, your wide shoulders, the way your hair shines in the moonlight, your soft lips, the way your brow furrows when you're deep in thought—"

I cut her off with a kiss, licking into her mouth and swallowing her words. Never have I felt so seen or so understood as I do with Nori, and it makes me ravenous for her.

"You ready for round two?" I rasp against her mouth.

Nori nods eagerly, then pauses. "Is this round three or four now? I'm losing count."

I hesitate. "Is that okay? We can stop if you want?"

Nori strokes first one cock, then the other. "No stopping until both your cocks fill my pussy with your cum."

The thought of that sight alone sends a visceral thrill through me. "Your wish is my command."

Not waiting a second longer, Nori notches my first cock at her entrance.

Carefully, I inch forward, breathing deeply as her soaked core envelops me, not wanting this to be over too soon.

When I'm fully seated, I take a moment to breathe, letting my forehead rest against Nori's. "You feel so good, Nori."

Once I feel like I have enough self-control again, I pull back and thrust forward, letting Nori get used to my cock.

"Shinsu," Nori mewls, and I already know what she needs.

The next time I pull back, Nori reaches between us and wraps two hands around my cocks, and guides them closer. When both heads kiss her slick opening, I take in a shuddering breath to brace myself for the pleasure that's to come.

"Look at you, my muse. The poems I can write about your cunt..." My words trail off as we both stare down at the place where we're joined, watching Nori's pussy stretching around my scaled cocks.

My eyes flick up to her eyes and she gives me an encouraging nod as I push forward a little bit more.

My whiskers reach for her sensitive clit, drawing circles around it, helping her relax as I work my way in.

The primal moan that comes out of Nori when our pelvises are flush together and both my cocks are fully sheathed, will forever be embedded in my memory.

I allow myself a short grunt as I hold absolutely still, keeping my body rigid, my breaths short and shallow, as I wait for Nori to adjust to my size.

Chest heaving, Nori opens her heavy-lidded eyes. "So full. Feels so good."

"Good?" I ask, needing to confirm that she loves this feeling as much as I do.

Nori nods stiffly. "Yes. Yes, yes, yes, yes, yes. Very. I want you like this all the time."

The breath that puffs out of me is pure elation. "Tell me when you're ready for me to move. I'll go slow."

"Now's good," Nori says as she rolls her hips into me.

I draw back then slowly advance again, giving Nori long, deep strokes that make her breath catch at the end of each one when I grind against her swollen clit. I monitor her carefully and gradually increase my pace when I can tell she's ready for more.

Soon, Nori's meeting each of my thrusts as I drive into her, her moans and mewls and whimpers forming a beautiful symphony with my own grunts and groans of pleasure.

Grabbing the back of her thigh, I lift her leg and prop her ankle on my shoulder so I can get even deeper. Then, my whiskers work their way in too. All of me filling Nori's tight cunt.

Nori throws her head back as her screams of ecstasy fill the room. She claws at me, marking me up, claiming me just as much as I'm claiming her.

My own pleasure sneaks up on me as I drive Nori toward another orgasm. "Nori, I'm close. Come with me."

Like she was waiting for the magical words, Nori's cunt clamps down on me, pulling me into the abyss of ecstasy with her. Ropes of cum burst from my cocks, filling Nori's sweet cunt over and over again.

Angling my horns to the side, I collapse onto the bed and roll us, draping Nori over me as we ride out the last remnants of our pleasure. Our chests heave in tandem as cum drips down from her and into my slit, filling me too with our combined releases.

I moan at the sensation as my whiskers retract from Nori and dive into our wet mess.

Nori lifts her head to stare down at me, a mischievous question in her eyes. "Is your slit sensitive?"

"Yes."

The corners of her mouth tip into a devious little smirk. "That's fun. I have a couple of ideas of what we can try next time."

Completely sated, I grin lazily back at her and tuck some curly copper strands behind her ear. "Whatever you want, it's yours."

"Do you think next time you can take my pussy with one cock while the other fucks my ass?"

My jaw drops and my hands still. "Yes. Very much, yes." My cocks start to harden again at the thought of claiming her ass too.

"And maybe one day I can try fucking your slit?"

I pause as I give that thought, but it doesn't take long until I'm nodding. "I think I'd really like that too."

Nori walks her fingers along the scales on my chest as she purrs, "Seems like we have a very adventurous future ahead of us."

"This is the best day of my life," I say, looking at my Nori with complete awe. "And yet the future looks even better with you by my side."

ELEANOR

CHAPTER 24

Standing in the middle of The Dancing Daisy, I turn in a circle to take it all in. Strong arms wrap around me and pull me against a hard chest.

"It's ready. You're ready," Shinsu says. I can't help thinking he's right.

I've kept most of the shop the same as Lucille had it, but I've added a fresh coat of paint, changing the sage-green accents to an aquamarine shade that reminds me of Shinsu.

The same orange leather chairs still sit in the reading corner and are now surrounded by a wider variety of magical candies, all of which Shinsu and I have explored together.

In the stationery section, I've added a few Knights and Castles materials too, including a wide selection of dice and other gaming props recommended by Shinsu. Plus, a sign-up sheet for anyone who wants to join their next campaign, which already has my name at the top of the list.

I rest my hands on Shinsu's arms and lean into him. "It has to be ready. Not like we can cancel the ribbon-cutting ceremony."

Shinsu turns me around and cups my shoulders. "If you tell me you want to cancel, I'll lock the door right now. Just give me the word."

Smiling up at my handsome dragon, I say, "And I'll love you for it. But I'm okay. I'm excited."

Like fate had timed those words, a knock sounds at the door. "Cake delivery!" Maisie says brightly as she waltzes in, Ren close on her heels as he carries the enormous cake, propping it up with his tail for extra balance.

"I love what you've done with the place," Maisie says as she turns in the center of the shop. Her gaze bounces over the stone walls and the shelves filled with a now much-expanded romance section before settling on the large calendar with its colorful markings. "Is this a community activity board?"

I walk over to Maisie while Shinsu shows Ren where to put the cake. "Thank you, and yes. I'll explain everything later in my speech, but I'm planning more events and opportunities for everyone to connect. My hope is that The Dancing Daisy will become a community hub where we can get together and do things we enjoy, maybe even learn a new skill or hobby." I point at the different days on the calendar as I explain, "We've already got the themed book clubs, and we'll do craft nights too for embroidery, crochet, and knitting. There will also be sip-and-paint evenings and book bedazzling. A little something for everyone. And so many of the locals have offered to lead events, so it's really a joint project on the hill and I'm just hosting."

Maisie bumps me with her shoulder. "Will you get annoyed with me if I sign up for all of them?"

I chuckle. "Not at all. I'm always happy to see you." And I mean that from the bottom of my heart.

Since moving to Starry Hill, I've felt happier and more fulfilled than I ever have before. I didn't realize how bad the quagmire of my life was before I became a part of the Starry Hill community. Here, they've breathed new life into me.

Especially Shinsu. Being loved by him is a gift. Going swimming with him at sunset every day is fun, either in his dragon form or his human form. Reading in my chair while he games with the boys on Saturdays is delightful. Eating his freshly baked bread and cooking dinner with him in the evenings is a dream.

Everything about our life together feels like a fairy tale and like I'm living in my happily ever after. Including waking up with him in the mornings, making slow, passionate love as the sun's rays filter into our home, or evenings where he fucks me so hard I scream until my voice is hoarse—it's all one giant adventure. A very happy one, at that.

Since I've been here, I've not had any contact with my mother. I've thrown away my straightener and had Beryl—Bodin's twin sister and owner of The Viny Shears, Starry Hill's barbershop and hair salon— teach me about curly hair care, following her advice and ordering the right products to look like my most authentic self.

Every day, I get to wear dresses, if I want. I love embracing my curves, and I love the way Shinsu loves them too. It's like I lived in the shadows for most of my life, and now I've finally found my way into the light.

Maisie takes both my hands in her. "I'm so happy you're here to stay. You've already made such a big impact on Starry Hill. And Beck." Cringing, Maisie smacks herself on the forehead. "Sorry, I mean Shinsu. I'm still getting used to calling him that, but isn't it just such a good name?"

I lower her hand and smile understandingly. "It's okay, and I agree. It's a beautiful name and suits him perfectly." Rubbing my thumb over the back of Maisie's hand, I think back to the reason I came to Starry Hill in the first place, feeling grateful for fate leading me here to help her open her cakery. "Thank you, Maisie. Thank you for welcoming me and making me feel a part of the community right from the start."

Narrowing her eyes playfully, Maisie shakes a warning finger at me. "You can't start with all the deep feelings so early in the day, or else we'll all be a crying mess before the main event. But let me just say, it wasn't hard by any means to befriend you. You slotted right into place here the moment you set foot on the island."

I'm about to reply with my thanks again, but Maisie forges ahead, slipping her arm through mine and dragging me toward the refreshment table. "Now let me show you the cake. We went with carrot because it was your favorite at your first ladies' night, but I added a bunch of stuff to it to make it more interesting—you've got a load of cinnamon, nutmeg, ginger, cloves, coconut flakes, raisins, chopped pecans, some pineapple juice, and then the best addition, a generous helping of spiced rum."

My mouth gapes open at the decadent two-tiered cake. "That does sound amazing. And it looks incredible. I love it all. Thank you so much."

"The pleasure is all mine." Maisie juts her chin toward Ren and Shinsu hanging out by the candy display. "Just look at our guys chatting and smiling so much. You know, not too long ago they were the quiet awkward ones on the island. I mean, they still have their oddities, and we love them for it, but they're no longer the outcasts living on the edge of the community. Look at them here at the center of it all, helping with the town's biggest event in ages."

My heart blossoms with her words, watching Shinsu smile and laugh with Ren, knowing he's loved and valued and integral to Starry Hill. There's a relaxed set to Shinsu's shoulders, a smile always lying in wait when he looks at me, and a lightness in his gaze now that he's at peace with his dragon.

Like the guys know we're talking about them, they come over, each of them slinging a possessive arm around our waists.

"Congratulations on the reopening of The Dancing Daisy," Ren says, perhaps a little shyly. "It looks new yet familiar. Refreshed is perhaps the best word."

I press a hand to my chest. "Thank you, Ren. The Daisy already has such a strong spirit, I didn't want to change her too much. But I'm excited for our future."

"I hope I'm included in this future," a sassy voice calls from the entrance.

My jaw drops as Audrey waltzes in with a giant bouquet of red roses. "Audrey. You're here."

"You didn't think I'd miss this, did you?" Audrey says as she draws me into a hug. Speaking over my shoulder, she passes Shinsu the flowers. "Be a doll and magic up some water for these, please."

My brain is still trying to catch up. "It's Friday. It's a work day."

Audrey shrugs as a sly smirk kicks up at the corner of her mouth. "So what if it is? I can take down the patriarchy any day of the week, but it's rare that one of your best friends opens her dream shop."

Tears fill my eyes, but before I can let them fall, Tilly waddles into the shop too, Bodin hovering close behind her.

"Oh, look. The gang's all here," Tilly says as she joins us, one hand cradling her growing stomach.

Audrey gives Tilly a quick once over. "Fucking hells, cousin. You okay?"

"Why wouldn't she be?" Bodin asks defensively.

"Because based on my research, her stomach is significantly bigger than what's to be expected at this point in her pregnancy." Turning to Tilly, she says placatingly, "But you look fantastic though. You're glowing. Never been more beautiful."

Maisie studies Tilly's rounded belly. "Is it because it's a half-orc baby and they're bigger than human babies?"

Tilly's eyes widen and she wobbles her head from side to side, not denying nor confirming Maisie's question.

Audrey gasps. "Don't tell me there are two in there."

Bodin puffs out his chest. "Twins run in our family."

"Holyyyy—"

"Damn—"

"Fucking—"

"Congratulations!" I raise my voice about the cacophony of expletives. "That's so exciting."

"And scary," Maisie says, knocking her knees together.

Shinsu looks down at me as he pulls me closer, keeping his voice low as he says, "Maybe soon we can also give them a little friend to play with?"

"Maybe," I say, knowing that plan isn't too far into the future. Shinsu and I both want a family with at least a couple of kids, and neither of us want to wait too long until we start trying.

For now though, we're enjoying each other and settling into our new life.

Lucille is next to arrive and I give her a private tour, showing her everything that I've kept exactly the same. I wait nervously for her approval when I show her the changes and the community board.

Lifting a wrinkly hand toward me, Lucille gives me a watery smile. "Eleanor dear, you're exactly what The Daisy needed. I knew she had a lot more to give, and you found a way to bring that forth."

I squeeze her hand gently. "I want to make you proud. And make our Daisy proud."

Lucille shakes her head. "My dear, you don't need my approval, even though you've always had it. The only person whose opinion matters here is yours. I hope you are so proud of yourself for how far you've come, how much you've grown, and how much you've given to our community."

Tilly inconspicuously hands me a handkerchief as she passes by, and I dab at my eyes, not wanting to ruin the little bit of makeup I have on today.

Soon, more creatures arrive, gathering outside the shop while my friends help me with some finishing touches. Shinsu, Ren, and Bodin hand out wrapped books to those in line, a little blind-date-with-a-book gift chosen from my list of personal favorites to those who are joining us.

By the time Arran—in full sunscreen protection—and Doc Calla arrive, everyone's buzzing with energy, ready to cut the giant orange ribbon and head inside to explore the shop.

Doc Calla, as the town's matriarch, gives me a heartwarming introduction and then it's time for my speech.

I swallow down my nerves and stand tall as I start speaking. "Thank you to everyone who's made it here today to celebrate the reopening of The Dancing Daisy with us. For decades, The Dancing Daisy has been a fixture in this community, and being entrusted with her means so much to me. The legacy of what

Lucille and her Lochan built here, with the guidance of his family before them, I promise to continue. My hope is that The Dancing Daisy will become a hub in this community, a safe space to connect with others, not only for the bibliophiles, but for anyone needing a friend or a new hobby to explore." I look toward Arran and dip my head at him, echoing this community's slogan that he made almost four hundred years ago. "Starry Hill—and The Dancing Daisy—welcome all."

Arran approaches me and shakes my hand. "Congratulations, Eleanor." Then, he hands me some very large antique-looking shears before melting back into the crowd.

I can't help but think of how many shop reopenings these shears have been a part of and how much history they've witnessed in this community. Getting to hold them too is an honor I don't take lightly.

Looking at everyone gathered in front of me, and Shinsu by my side, a smile stretches across my face as I angle the shears against the orange fabric. Cheers resound from the crowd as the ribbon separates and flutters to the ground, amplifying the exhilarated feeling rushing through my veins.

My heart swells as creatures slowly funnel into my shop, smiles and words of encouragement on their lips.

I lean against Shinsu as I watch them head to different sections, many of them pointing out changes I've made, and a large group lingering around the community board, discussing which events to sign up for.

I couldn't have imagined a more perfect day.

Shinsu presses a kiss to my head. "You did it, Nori. You made your own dream come true. I know you don't need to hear it from me, but I'm so proud of you."

I wrap my arms around Shinsu's waist and stare up at his beautiful face and the two pearlescent horns glinting in the sun. "Thank you. I don't think I would've been brave enough to do this without you. Your support, all the planning sessions, the late nights we've worked together, the numerous trips into the city to get the right stock, it means so much to me."

Shinsu cradles my face, his thumb brushing across my cheek. "You're very welcome. I'll always be here to help you with anything you need."

"Well, since you're offering..."

"Yes?"

I flutter my eyelashes at him, pretending this is a new idea and that I haven't been practicing in secret over the past few weeks. "Can we go to The Singing Seahorse tonight? I have a little surprise for you. Just a small thank-you for everything."

Shinsu's eyes widen, anticipation building behind them. "Are you going to sing karaoke?"

I try my best to give him a nonchalant shrug, fighting off my blush that he's already figured out my plan. "You'll just have to wait and see. Now let's head inside and celebrate this day with our community."

Shinsu laces our fingers together. "You lead the way."

Every night when I go to sleep, I think that day was the best day of my life. So far, each day has only gotten better, but it's certainly going to be hard to top today as my current number one.

Epilogue

Audrey

Scooting into the booth next to Calixta and Beryl, I keep one eye on The Singing Seahorse's crowd, wondering if there are any single creatures here tonight who might tickle my fancy. Or other body parts. Hopefully other body parts.

"Is everyone on this island happily coupled up?" I sigh out, then take a long sip of my cocktail.

Calixta's topaz eyes brighten. "Not everyone. What's your poison? I'll tell you if they're worth the hunt."

My upper lip curls back. "Girl, I don't hunt. I'm a prey worthy of pursuit," I say, flipping my short hair off my shoulder.

Beryl chuckles and pulls her wife into her side. "It's good that you know what you like and don't like. It makes finding a good partner a very rewarding experience." There's heavy innuendo in the statement, and it makes Calixta's tail curl tighter around Beryl's thigh, almost disappearing underneath her skirt.

I shift my gaze away from the happy couple and back toward the stage where Marisol is wrapping up her romantic serenade for her three partners. *Seriously, I get no one and she gets to have three? It sucks that the siren is so nice and so pretty and totally deserves all the orgasms.*

My brain finally registers what Beryl said. "Uhm, I don't do partners. I'm perfectly happy on my own. I'm just looking for... entertainment. Of the sexual kind. Maybe some light, short-term companionship. Preferably not lasting more than a single night. Two tops."

Calixta smirks. "Weirdly, that narrows down your options."

"What? How?"

Scooting closer to me, Calixta lowers her voice just enough for my human ears to hear. "Well, take Aurelius there, for example," she says, angling her adorned horns toward the guy with large white wings and a golden shirt unbuttoned past his chest. "The mothman is single, but he's a little hung up on Peregrine. If you were to catch his eye instead, get ready for total obsession. He's like a dog with a bone."

A shudder rolls through me. "Nope. Too intense. Next."

Beryl pauses with her beer halfway to her mouth. "There's Pierre, the gargoyle. He's really grumpy and I've not known him to take any partners since... well, ever."

Calixta shakes her head, making the draped beads around her horns clink with motion. "I don't think he's your cup of tea. Pierre is the one complaining whenever we can't wait to get home and head into an alley to..."

Beryl places a green finger against Calixta's black lips. "She gets the point, my heart."

I shoot them a finger gun. "So, no alley sex. Got it."

Calixta and Beryl proceed to tell me about other singles in town and what's wrong with them, dashing my hopes for some fun, one creature at a time.

"There's always Arran," Beryl suggests cautiously. "We haven't mentioned him yet."

That gets my attention because I'm pretty sure we made eye contact at The Dancing Daisy's opening this morning. "I think I saw him earlier. Is he the hottie with the vintage shirt and cropped hair?"

Beryl almost spits out her drink as she starts to laugh. "That's him, yes. And what you call a vintage shirt is what Arran simply calls a shirt. He doesn't get out of his castle much. He's a bit of a homebody."

I lean forward on my elbow and rest my chin in my hand. "Castle, you say? Go on."

"Founder of Starry Hill, about four hundred years old—" Calixta ticks off the attributes on her fingers, but I don't let her finish.

"Ouch," I hiss. "Talk about an age gap." Seeing an opportunity for something I haven't tried before, I cock a brow at them. "Do you think he'd like it if I called him daddy?"

Beryl's denial is quick. "Definitely not."

Her wife, though, has a different opinion. "Maybe you should try it."

I sigh and flop back in the booth. "Would if I could. But it's not like I can simply waltz over to his place, knock on his castle door, and shout 'Daddy, come ravish me.'" It would definitely make for a good introduction, if he was into it. But would I be? Always good to try something at least once.

Snickering, Beryl says, "I'd pay big money to see that."

"Maybe—" My words cut off as the crowd cheers and Eleanor heads to the stage.

I've attended a couple of karaoke nights and ladies' night since Tilly moved to Starry Hill, but never have I seen Eleanor do anything that draws attention to herself.

This morning at The Dancing Daisy's reopening, it must've taken a lot of courage from Eleanor to give a speech in front of a crowd that size, so seeing her on stage here with even more people makes me excited for her, and very curious.

Eleanor taps the microphone once to check that it's on. "Hi, everyone. I, uhm... This song is dedicated to the love of my life, Shinsu Beck. I've known him since I was seven, and even though we didn't see each other for more than two decades, I can promise you that I never forgot him. Nor this song."

Marisol cues a familiar tune that I recognize as the same one Shinsu always performs and gives Eleanor two thumbs-up. All eyes turn to him as he watches Eleanor with rapt attention, his jaw agape and eyes wide.

Eleanor starts what seems to be a choreographed dance then begins singing, shyly at first, but her confidence grows as the crowd cheers her on. Even though she's nervous, she's smiling and having the time of her life.

Less than a minute into the song, Shinsu rushes to the stage and picks up the second microphone. The goofy grins that beam out of them as they fall into rhythm with each other, harmonizing and dancing in perfect tune with each other, makes me oddly emotional.

I knew they had a strong connection, but witnessing it in action like this almost makes me wish for my own someone to share my life with. Almost. But not quite.

Ew. Where did that thought come from?

The song finishes and everyone cheers, wild applause resounding from the entire pub as we realize Shinsu had always performed that song as an ode to their friendship and now Eleanor has finally made it come full circle.

Talk about yearning over the decades.

I shudder just to think what that level of love would feel like. I'm sure it comes with a lot of baggage to sort through before you get to have this level of happiness again.

"You going back to Cape Easton tonight?" Beryl asks once the noise has died down.

"Uhm, I don't think that's happening." I point at Shinsu's ravenous gaze as he steers Eleanor away from the stage and straight to the front door. "Something's telling me I should avoid the dock tonight. Or being anywhere in those two's vicinity for the next couple of hours. Good for them though."

Calixta cracks her neck and shakes her long red limbs as if to rid herself of something. "Let me tell you, being a succubus in this town was almost boring before I got married. But lately... let's just say I'm glad I'm well-fed at home, otherwise the sexual energy pumping through this room would have me in a state." Calixta points a long black nail at Marisol, Bash, Killian, and Silas and their very obvious eye fucking and not-so-subtle touching behind the counter. She angles her hand in another direction and points at Tilly sitting on Bodin's lap and his hand splayed across her ass. Then, she shifts over to Viggo and Juniper, Maisie and Ren, plus Aurelius and Peregrine—the final two thinking no one can make out where their hands are in the dark corner in the back of the pub.

"I'm fucked," I say with a pout, realizing my attempt at finding some fun is completely futile.

"I think you're the opposite of fucked," Beryl counters and snorts into her beer.

Clinking my glass to hers, I say, "Can't argue with that fact. At least I always carry a tiny toy for times of extreme need." I lift the long silver chain around my neck and show them the elegant silver vibrator clipped to it.

Beryl's gaze darkens as she looks at Calixta. "Now that's interesting."

Tail now hidden under Beryl's skirt and with sexual energy so strong even I can feel it, Calixta rasps, "Do you have somewhere you can stay tonight?" The succubus doesn't fully glance my way, her eyes trained hungrily on her wife instead.

With my ability to read the room, I'm already scooting out the booth. "Yeah, I'll crash at Bodin's old apartment above The Bandaged Heart. Won't be the first time I've used the empty space. I'll catch a lift with Viggo into the city in the morning once he and Juniper resurface from their nightly love nest."

They wave goodbye before they're heading out the door, a sense of urgency driving their feet as I flit between tables and strike up new conversations with my friends.

Very soon, the other couples' energies change too, hands disappearing under tables as they exchange loaded looks.

Eventually, I say my goodbyes, and my trusty necklace and I head down the darkened hill toward First Street and the little apartment above Tilly's clinic.

Before Tilly and Bodin's sunrise wedding, I stayed here for a night to ensure I could help her get ready in plenty of time. I've also crashed here a time or two after ladies' night when I didn't want to bother someone to ferry me home so late.

Before I can get the door fully open, a particularly hairy man sticks his head around it, and I just manage to muffle my scream.

"What do you want?" he hisses at me.

I look behind me then back at him. "What do I want? Who are you?"

"The new tenant," he says with a tilt to his chin.

"What? Since when?"

The guy huffs. "That's none of your business."

"True." I blow out a long breath. "Sorry for disturbing you. No one told me there was someone living here. I usually crash here when I'm in town."

The hairy guy sticks his head out a little further and takes a surreptitious glance down the street. "I'm keeping a low profile," he whispers. "Not many people know I'm here. Do you have somewhere else to go?"

"Uhm..."

"How about Arran's place?" he offers enthusiastically. "He's very nice and I'm sure he wouldn't mind putting you up."

I narrow my eyes at the stranger. "You know what? You're not the first creature to suggest that tonight."

"Good. We have to follow the signs," he practically hisses again before shutting the door.

Still in shock and very much confused, I stare at the closed door. "Okayyy... Nice to meet you, dude. Bye."

So, I find myself walking across Starry Hill in the middle of the night, guided only by the stars above me and my need to find a bed for a couple of hours.

It doesn't take long before the highest tower of the castle pierces the eastern horizon. Relief fills me at the sight and I quickly check my watch to calculate the timing of my next shot of insulin. The last thing I want to do is stress my soon-to-be host by going hyperglycemic.

I stop in front of the gigantic door, noticing that not one light is turned on in the castle.

Maybe he's asleep already? In that case, I might just be able to slip in unnoticed, and perhaps even leave by morning light without him realizing I was even here.

Why do I feel nervous about it? No one's going to know.

My hand lands on the antique knob and I hesitate before I push against the door with my shoulder.

I cringe as an eerie creek rings through the quiet night as the door slowly swings open.

When I look up, Arran is standing in front of me, hands on hips and looking way too good for my hungry pussy.

"Hi," I say, giving him a cute wave.

Arran scowls at me and I wish I didn't find grumpy men so attractive. "Why are you here?"

"Uhm, can we have a sleepover?" I ask, giving my best impression of a doe-eyed look.

The scowl deepens, with a little bit of confusion creeping in too. "A what?"

"I'm staying the night and will be gone in the morning," I say quickly, patting his hard chest as I step into the dark castle.

"I... uhm... you..."

Turning back toward him, I point over my shoulder at the colossal staircase. "Which way is my bedroom?"

Arran blankly lifts his hand and points to the right.

"Thanks, stud." I blow him a kiss then skip up the stairs, ready for my first night in a castle.

Something tells me this is going to be lots of fun.

Want to know what'll happen with Arran and Audrey? Get ready for their story in the final book in the Creatures & Cottages series — *The Vampire's Darling,* coming summer 2026.

Need some bonus content? Subscribe to my newsletter to stay up to date on my publishing news.

Acknowledgments

Thank you so much for reading The Dragon's Muse and being patient with Shinsu and Nori as they found their happy ending. If you enjoyed this book, please consider leaving a rating or review so other readers can discover their story too.

This was one of my most challenging books to write, not only because it dealt with heavier themes, but also due to the current state of the world and its effect on my mental health. The more I wrote, the more I realized how much I need my own community, and this echoed into Nori's story too. This book became my love letter to those in my life who lift me up and give me a safe space to simply be myself.

So often when we're adults we think we need to have it all figured out, but many of us are still struggling through our lives with a little bit (or a lot) of baggage. It was important to me that Nori found a group of friends and a job she loved as well as finding a partner who understands and supports her. And for everyone who's been championing Shinsu from when Beck was introduced in book 1, thank you for sticking around and giving my awkward dragon so much love.

I really wanted to feature a dragon based on Korean mythology and I was so excited when Beck's character popped into my head for this first time. My husband helped me brainstorm names that suited our water dragon and translated well into English too—if you haven't noticed from my books, I'm pretty obsessed with the meaning of names. And so, Shinsu's lore started. I loved adding a few subtle nods to Korean culture and the language along the way as another little love note to the country I call home.

This story would never have found its happy ending without the help of a few people very dear to me.

Adrienne, you had to read through almost triple the book with all the rewrites I did. Thank you for being patient with me and steering me in the right direction when I needed it.

Lanae, thank you for all the voice notes, the reactions, the advice, plus helping me design Shinsu's very unique peen.

Impyeu, once again you blew me away. The blue-and-orange sunset will forever be one of my favorite covers you've done.

Lindsey, Colette, Laura, Meg, Monika, Elle, and McKayla—thank you for always being in my DMs and holding my hand when I need it most.

My street team, aka the Starry Hill Smut Club, I love you and appreciate you. Thank you for helping me share my stories with the world.

But most importantly, thank you, dear reader, for choosing one of my books. Your support means the world to me.

—Elle

Also by Elle Sterling

MONSTERS OF ALBERAD

Tempting the Dhampir

Enchanting the Elf

Courting the Krampus

CREATURES & COTTAGES

The Orc's Sweetheart

The Incubus's Angel

The Dragon's Muse

The Vampire's Darling (Summer 2026)

NOVELLAS

Party With the Kraken

Halloween With the Siren

About the Author

Elle Sterling is an author of wholesomely horny romance that'll make you giggle and swoon.

Much like her own life after emigrating from South Africa to South Korea, she enjoys writing characters crossing cultural barriers and loving without restraint.

You can usually find Elle in her writing cave with coffee within reach at all times. She also enjoys grilled kimchi-and-cheese sandwiches and hibernates during the humid summer until the weather has cooled.

Elle loves connecting with readers, so visit her on social media (@ellesterlingauthor) or email her: elle@ellesterling.com